ABLAZE

ABLAZE

Christopher Krovatin

Scholastic Inc.

Copyright © 2023 by Christopher Krovatin

All rights reserved. Published by Scholastic Inc., *Publishers since 1920*. SCHOLASTIC and associated logos are trademarks and/or registered trademarks of Scholastic Inc.

The publisher does not have any control over and does not assume any responsibility for author or third-party websites or their content.

This book is a work of fiction. Names, characters, places, and incidents are either the product of the author's imagination or are used fictitiously, and any resemblance to actual persons, living or dead, business establishments, events, or locales is entirely coincidental.

ISBN 978-1-338-81603-7

10 9 8 7 6 5 4 3 2 1   23 24 25 26 27

Printed in the U.S.A.   40

First printing 2023

Book design by Christopher Stengel

FOR ANNA QUINDLEN, MOTHER OF THREE,
FOREVER PUTTING OUT FIRES AND
FANNING SPARKS

SPARK

Heat. Pain. Burned skin.

Aly yanked her hand back from the oven and shook it. She'd gotten distracted by a crash from Rachael's room upstairs, and her knuckle had glanced the middle rack. *Careless*, she told herself. She used two wadded-up dish towels to pull the muffins out, then ran her knuckle under a cold tap. The water felt good, but the steady sting of the burn never quite went away.

"Aw, I was going to do that!" cried Mom as she came into the kitchen. She was dressed for action, Aly noticed—sweatpants, sneakers, hair pulled back.

"It's fine. I can handle it," said Aly. "Need a hand with Simon?"

Mom exhaled and pinched the bridge of her nose. "Actually, yeah, that would be a big help." She shot Aly an exhausted smile. "You cool, kiddo?"

"I'm cool," said Aly. She smiled big, her braces unabashedly on full display. These days, only a few people got that smile, and Mom was one of them.

Her hand still burned as she put a couple of muffins on a plate and brought them down the hall to Simon's room. Sometimes, as the middle kid, she wondered if she was even here at all, if anyone actually *saw* her around the house. But you couldn't daydream away tying someone's shoes or bringing them breakfast.

Simon sat on his bed in his socks and pants, but had no shirt or shoes on. Aly could see by the look in his eyes that his mind was far away, playing out some long, complicated conversation. Her breath hitched in her throat; when he got like this, it always made her momentarily sick with worry, wondering what her little brother was seeing that she couldn't. But he'd done it enough times that Aly knew he was just lost in his thoughts.

"Simon," she said, and gently waved a muffin under his nose. He came to, his nine-year-old humanity returning to his face. He took the muffin and had a bite, but she could tell he was still lost in his own head. "What's up, man?"

"What do I do about Bentley?" asked Simon softly.

Aly bit her own muffin and nodded. Bentley Moss was the kid in the grade above Simon's who'd been bothering him. She knew the right answer was to tell her brother to talk to a teacher . . . but she couldn't say it out loud and feel honest about it. Not with her own ongoing issues with Ray.

"Try to think about what he's feeling," she said. "Like, what's going on in his life to make him such a mean guy?"

"I *know* what he's feeling," said Simon. "He's just angry at everything. And I'm easy pickings."

Aly sighed. Couldn't argue with that.

"Well, look, no matter what happens with that jerk, you're going to look silly at school without a shirt and shoes on," she said. "So let's get dressed, and we can think about a way to avoid Bentley Moss on the drive."

Simon nodded absently and went to get a shirt from his dresser. Aly sat on his bed and gave him little reminders along the way—"You should double-knot that. Do you need that notebook? Remember what Mom said about that thing in the printer." She loved him so much, but she also worried for him.

Comes with being the youngest, she thought to herself as she led her brother to the front hallway. *There's always someone around to do stuff for you* . . .

There was the bang of a door being thrown open, and a forceful whisper of "Let's just do this."

And that's what comes with being the eldest, thought Aly, exhausted.

Rachael came clomping downstairs. Aly took in the outfit—designer jeans, a cute maroon blouse, an extra-tight hoodie with ENGLAND across the chest, magenta lip gloss, shades, and crisp white high-top sneakers. It had been assembled over time, she realized, each piece an expensive birthday or Christmas gift that had apparently all led up to this Monday morning. That was Rachael all over—obsessed with being popular, hardworking and strategic when it came to getting the coolest friends, the most followers, and the hottest reputation in school.

"Are we GOING SOON?" yelled Rachael into the house. She lowered her sunglasses and looked over them at Aly. "Can I help you, Als?"

"No," said Aly. "You look nice."

"That's great, Als, except we're late, so I might as well have worn a large cloth *sack*." Rachael groaned. "I had this whole thing planned out, where I would be wearing this while sitting on the banister of the front steps, and *a certain someone* would *see me* as he walked into school, and it would be this perfect *vignette* that would inspire him to ask me to the April Showers Dance. But by the time we get there, what I know about that *someone's* schedule tells me that he will probably already *be there*, so the whole thing is a *mess*."

Your priorities are a mess, Rach, thought Aly, but she decided to consider her sister's problem as though it were an actual problem. Calling Rachael out never got her anywhere.

"You could go for much more of a strutting-in-confidently, I-know-I-look-good kind of thing," she said. "That always works in the movies. Like, he's hanging with his boys, you enter in slo-mo, he notices you out of the corner of his eye—*Wow, who's that?*"

"Classic," said Simon.

Rachael slowly began to nod and sucked air between her teeth. "That is not a bad way to turn this around. This is why we pay you the big bucks, Als." She smelled the air. "Did Mom make muffins? Oh my God, I'm STARVING."

As she tromped off to the kitchen, Dad finally came downstairs, fixing his tie. "Everyone ready? Rumor is we're in a hurry."

"When I'm done eating!" shouted Rachael from the kitchen.

When they pulled up to school, Rachael got out of the car before Dad could even start saying goodbye. She brushed herself down, looked back at Aly, gave her a nod, and marched off toward school.

Aly looked down at her hand. Her burn from the

oven was swollen, irritated. A small white blister had formed on it.

Nobody had noticed. Not even Dad.

The front lawn of their private day school was a blur of various crews of kids chatting noisily—the lacrosse guys talking about last night's game, doing hand gestures and then slapping five; the golden-haired horse girls giggling excitedly over a new country song they'd just heard, including Jess Gregor, who'd been Aly's best friend before she got cool; the hunched goths with their oversized hoodies and green highlights, blasting morbid music from their phones; the junior fashionistas, looking bored in their influencer poses, Rachael among them rolling her eyes in conversation with her friend Martina.

Aly moved past them all, part of no tribe, doing her best to keep her head down. It was the only way she knew how to get by.

Be invisible, and no one even thinks to pick on you. It had done her well so far.

Well, sort of.

"Heads up, Theland!"

She barely registered the call before her foot landed on the skateboard and everything went topsy-turvy. Aly went weightless for one moment before collapsing hard on her side with a cry. All around her, the lawn echoed with kids going, "OOOOOH!"

"Are you all right?" asked Simon, bending down to try to help her up.

Aly nodded as she got to her feet; her ankle felt sore and her hip stung, but she was fine. Mostly what hurt was her pride. Her cheeks burned as she noticed how many pairs of eyes were pinned on her.

This wasn't how she'd wanted to finally be seen.

Even she had to admit, invisibility wasn't working.

Most of her life, she'd been able to swallow it down . . . but right now, a small part of her imagined flipping out on everyone, whipping her backpack overhead, and throwing it at the nearest window. About running across the lawn, knocking down a lacrosse boy, kicking Jess's shin. Lately, she felt like she was going to burst, having bottled up so many of her feelings and opinions for the sake of going along, keeping the peace, staying unnoticed. Sometimes, it was like all she could hear was a harsh noise in her head, like silverware scraping plates, until she thought she might just go sprinting through town shrieking, *Look at me. LOOK AT ME. I'M NOT NEARLY AS COOL WITH ALL THIS AS I TELL MY MOM I AM—*

"God, Theland, watch where you're going." Ray Westra loped in front of her and kicked the board up into his hand. He smirked at her from beneath his Supreme cap. "I let my board slip and *of course* you find a way to trip on it. Get it together."

She watched Ray walk off, snickering and shaking his head to himself, and felt the heat in her cheeks surge. She wished she could make a meteorite come shooting out of space and crush Ray. She wished she could make a hole open up in the earth to swallow him.

"Do you know that guy?" asked Simon.

"Yeah," mumbled Aly through the haze of her rage. "He's my lab partner."

The entire day, she dreaded chemistry, desperate to do anything other than relive the humiliation of the morning. But her fall in front of everyone followed her everywhere, people mumbling, *Rachael Theland's sister totally ate it* or *Ray says she's a klutz, anyway.*

When she got to the science lab after lunch, Ray was one of the people already there, setting up beakers full of various solutions. The sight of him made her stop in her tracks. She seriously considered just running away, but she forced herself to walk over to their shared table. *He's some guy in ripped jeans and a hoodie*, she told herself. *He's no one to get all upset over.*

"What do I need to set up?" she asked, trying to sound cheerful.

"My board is probably super messed up from you stomping on it today," Ray responded loudly. Even their teacher, Mr. Chalnak, glanced up from the board and looked at them.

Aly took a deep breath, trying to stay calm. "Then you shouldn't have let it roll out into the path—"

"You have to speak up if you're going to talk to people," Ray interrupted, rolling his eyes. "Must be all that metal crap in your mouth. Anyway, hope your folks are rich. That's a custom deck." He glared at her and smirked. "Though with what you're wearing, I doubt that's the case."

Aly felt her mouth go tight as she tried to keep the crashing noises at bay. *Being angry won't help*, she told herself. *He does this EVERY DAY, and any time you get upset, he makes you out to be the jerk. Just ignore him.*

"Let me help get the test tubes in the rack," she mumbled, and reached over for them—

Ray smacked her hand away, right on her burn.

Aly yanked her hand back, stunned, and hissed through her teeth.

Her mind was a cloud of white static. Outrage. Disbelief. *Pain.*

Had he actually slapped her hand away?

"You stick to the paperwork," Ray said. "This morning proved you're clumsy. You've ruined enough of my stuff for one day."

But Aly couldn't hear his words anymore. All she could hear was a great rushing noise in her mind, like a volcano inside her had erupted and was spilling white-hot lava across her entire being. She'd put up with Ray's thinly veiled sexism and his insults about her braces and even the comments about her "hot" sister or "weird" brother, but now he'd actually touched

her; he'd actually *SLAPPED HER HAND AWAY,*
AND THAT
WAS
ENOUGH.

Ray cried out and dropped the beaker in his hand. It hit their table and shattered, sending blue liquid across the table.

The liquid was on fire.

All the fluid in all the beakers was on fire, sending jets of flame into the air, making glass shatter with their heat.

Though she was frightened, and though she could faintly hear her classmates shouting and Mr. Chalnak screaming for the fire extinguisher, all Aly could do was look at Ray's face, open-mouthed with terror and surrounded by a halo of flames.

KINDLING

"Is this your first time here?"

Aly's eyes snapped up from the poster of a kitten next to a pile of books (READING—IT'S THE CAT'S PAJA-MAS! said the caption in big green letters). Principal Winters smiled at her from behind his desk, looking tired and a little confused but not very threatening.

"Yes," admitted Aly.

"See, that's what I thought," said the principal. "From what I've read, you're a pretty good kid, Aly.

No trouble. That's why I figured I ought to meet with you after what happened today, just to make sure you're the kind of kid I thought you'd be. I wasn't very moved by Raymond Westra's story."

She nodded and dry-swallowed. The image of Ray's freaked-out face still hung in her mind; over time, it went from making her feel excited and empowered to making her feel sick and worried about whether or not he was okay. She'd been *so* angry . . .

"What did Ray say?" she asked.

Principal Winters shrugged and rolled his eyes. "Apparently, you flung flammable chemicals on him and tossed a lit match. Says you did it to get revenge on him for"—he checked the screen of his computer—"pushing his skateboard in front of you before school, and tripping you up. Which I'm sure he did. And Mr. Chalnak already told me that. Heck, he even said that none of the chemicals were that flammable, so it had to be some sort of freak accident." He smiled and shrugged again. "And, well . . . let's just say that our friend Raymond knows the inside of this room a lot better than you do. If we figure out what happened, we'll tell you. Otherwise, you're free to go."

Aly felt like a criminal walking out of the princi-pal's office, even though she knew that was silly. She just wasn't used to being in any kind of trouble. She'd never even gotten detention before. Now she was frightened about losing her anonymity. The idea of people around their school talking about her, making up rumors about her, acting like they knew her was really nerve-racking.

She was so deep in her thoughts, she almost ran into Jess Gregor. Her ex-friend stood in front of her with her arms folded, leaning against a locker.

"Excuse me," Aly mumbled. She moved to her right—but Jess stepped into her path, blocking her. Aly forced herself to meet Jess's eyes. Her old friend looked so different now, she thought, her face slathered with makeup and her neck bearing a pair of thick, expen-sive Bluetooth headphones. Her head was tilted slightly back so that she seemed to be eyeing Aly from some great height as if Aly was a bug under Jess's shoe.

"What, Jess?" Aly asked, giving a little shrug as though to say, *I don't have time for this.*

"I heard you set Ray Westra on fire in the science lab today," said Jess with a smirk.

Aly heard a giggle and spotted two of Jess's new friends, Athena Heralda and Kristy Schnapp, huddled and whispering a few feet away. Her heart sank and her eyes stung as she realized what was going on here. Jess was making a show of her social superiority. She was picking on the freak because it was a freak she knew.

"That's not what happened," said Aly. "Now I have to—" But when she darted back toward the lockers, Jess moved to block her path again. A few feet away, Athena snickered.

"I heard you stood over him and laughed," Jess went on. "Is *that* true? Are you some kind of pyro?"

Aly felt her lips draw tight, felt her hands clench around the straps of her backpack, felt a tightness building in her head—

A hand slammed into the lockers between them. Both Aly and Jess jumped with a gasp.

Rachael leaned forward and stink-eyed Jess. Aly's big sister was only three or four inches taller than the girl, but the way she stood and peered at her made Jess look three feet shorter. Now it was Jess who was the bug—even someone as out of touch as Aly knew that

Rachael outranked Jess popularity-wise, which was obviously a concern of Jess's these days.

"*I heard* that your mom lost her mind at a Whole Foods cashier and had to be escorted out by security, Gregor," said Rachael, loudly enough for Jess's friends and any passersby to hear it. "But you don't see me or my sister blocking your way and telling you about it, do you?"

Jess's mouth opened and closed. Her eyes flitted between Aly and Rachael. "I—I—"

"You what?" asked Rachael. Jess looked down at the ground and shook her head. "Yeah. Weird that you thought *now* would be an okay time to start talking to my sister again. Come on, Als, let's go."

Rachael put her arm over Aly's shoulder and steered her away from Jess. Aly was stunned. Her heart was a storm of emotions—embarrassment, surprise . . . but also pride. Rachael had never stuck up for her before, and certainly not like this.

"I could've handled that myself," she said softly.

"I know," said Rachael. "But you shouldn't have to."

Heat bloomed once more inside Aly—but it was a

different kind of flush this time, more powerful than being angry at Jess.

"Thanks, Rachael," she said.

Aly's older sister shrugged and looked at her nails. "Any time. I was just passing by, anyway."

"Please excuse my dear Aunt Sally," mumbled Aly. "Please excuse my . . . *ugh*!"

Aly sat back and rubbed at her eyes. It was no use—no matter how much she tried to focus on the order of operations, she couldn't concentrate. It was like her mind refused to let her finish her homework until she thought about what had happened in the science lab that afternoon. Until it once again pictured Ray's shocked face, shouts coming from all around her, the smell of the chemicals, the shattering glass . . .

The fire.

It was all she could think about. When she replayed the accident in her mind, that's what always hit her first: the dancing light of the flames, the heat of them against her face, the way they spread across the table in a blue wave that blossomed into orange petals. The fire had been scary . . . but it had also been beautiful.

Or maybe not *beautiful*. Maybe *powerful*.

After the morning she'd had—making muffins because Mom was too busy, rousing Simon from his distraction, tripping over Ray's skateboard—she had felt completely helpless, crushed under the weight of the world, punished for nothing. The flames moving across the surface of the lab table felt like her emotions had manifested themselves physically. She had felt a fire inside her, and then there it was, on the table, billowing toward Ray, searing her cheeks, and making the room smell like burning paper . . .

Aly blinked and tried to shake the thought out of her head. Maybe Jess was right. Was this what pyromaniacs did—sat around and thought about fire all night?

"*Ugh*," she repeated, and went back to her homework. The order of operations. Please excuse my dear Aunt Sally. That meant she had to do the math problem with parentheses, exponents . . . multipliers? And then what was the D?

She'd never get it. She wasn't even smart enough to be a *nerdy* outcast; she was just a nobody.

Ray was right about you, she thought.

A shadow seemed to appear in the center of the math problem on her notebook page.

Before Aly knew what was happening, the shadow grew, and a glowing orange dot appeared in its middle.

Then, with a *fwump*, fire poured out of it, engulfing her desk.

COMBUSTION

Aly leaped to her feet, knocking her chair over. For a second, she wondered if she was imagining this, maybe having some sort of flashback to this afternoon. Then she felt the flames lick at her face and smelled the stink of her hair getting singed.

The flames were real. Her desk was burning . . . and the fire was getting bigger.

Aly's lips quivered. Her head darted around the room. She had no idea what to do. She tried to move, but she couldn't take her eyes away from the column of fire that was erupting from her desk, the twisting orange and flickering yellow, the way it devoured everything beneath it . . .

"Hey, Aly, Simon needs you to— OH MY GOD!" Aly whirled to see her siblings standing in her doorway, their eyes huge as they watched her desk go up in flames. Rachael waved her hands wildly near her chest while Simon stood rigid, his mouth frozen in an O shape.

"HELP!" screamed Aly, tears stinging her eyes.

Both of Aly's siblings broke out of their trances and ran in opposite directions—Simon turned and fled down the hall while Rachael barreled into Aly's room and yanked a quilt from her bed. She began beating at the flames with the blanket, trying to put them out, but all it seemed to do was send pieces of burnt notebook flying through the air.

"THIS ISN'T WORKING!" shrieked Aly.

"I'M TRYING!" Rachael shouted back, and soon the girls were both screaming at once, their voices reaching a piercing pitch of panic that seemed to blend seamlessly with the shrieking beep of the smoke detector outside Aly's door—

FSSSSSH. A white, chemical-smelling powder blasted onto the flames, immediately dousing them. Aly and Rachael backed away, coughing and waving their hands in front of their faces. As the dust cloud diminished, Simon appeared out of the cloud, his body heaving with breath. His arms shook from holding up the fire extinguisher.

"Oh my God!" The Theland siblings all turned with a start. Mom stood at the door with her hands clapped over her mouth.

The smoke detector cut out, and Dad followed behind her and mumbled, "Whoa." As Aly felt her panic subside a little, she surveyed the damage and understood why her parents were so upset. Everything on one side of her bedroom was coated in a thick layer of white fireproof powder. Her desk was blackened all over, with slow wisps of smoke rising from its charred surface. Her math notebook was burned to a crisp, barely recognizable.

"It's okay," said Aly, breathing fast, her mind and heart racing. "We put it out."

"Put it— Aly, what *happened* here?" her mom asked.

Aly did her best to think fast. She tried to come up with an answer that wasn't *I got angry and set it on fire with my mind*. What could she possibly say?

It was Simon who spoke instead. "It . . . must have been my . . . strike-anywhere matches."

Aly's brow furrowed, and she slowly turned to look at Simon. Her little brother was frozen, the fire extinguisher dangling from his hands.

"What does *that* mean?" asked Mom.

To be fair, thought Aly, *I'm wondering the same thing*.

"I . . . have a project for social studies," said Simon, his confused facial expression telling Aly that he was making his whole story up on the spot. "About things that people don't make anymore, but . . . were popular." He dry-swallowed and nodded, as though to himself. "Aly told me she found some strike-anywhere matches in Grampa's stuff in the basement. I thought that'd be cool . . . but she said she wanted to hold on to them for me. Because they're dangerous. You hit them wrong, and they go off. She must have accidentally set them off." Simon looked pleadingly at Aly. "Right?"

Aly was dumbfounded by Simon's lie. She felt the

eyes of the room on her, waiting for her to say something. She shot a quick glance to Rachael, who gave her a half shrug as though to say, *Do you have anything better?*

"It must have been those matches," Aly said. "I was frustrated with my homework, so I slammed my hand down on the desk . . . and I must have set them off."

"Simon actually mentioned these to me," said Rachael. "Another kid in his class is bringing in a bottle of Crystal Pepsi, so he wanted to top her."

Dad looked confused but seemed to buy the story. Not Mom, though—Aly could see by her hard gaze that she was trying to root out the truth behind the fib. But for the first time in her life, Aly held her tongue from her mother. Even their middle-child bond didn't make Aly want to reveal the actual story.

Especially because she didn't quite believe it herself.

Finally, Mom let her arms flop down at her sides. "Well . . . I guess you'll have to be more careful in the future. And you can sleep in Rachael's room until we clean things up. You're sure you're okay?"

"Yeah," Aly said. "I'm cool, Mom. I'm fine."

Mom turned and went off to get some cleaning supplies, with Dad following close behind.

The minute they were out of earshot, Rachael turned to Aly with a tired smile.

"Okay, so, lesson one," she said, "Simon doesn't come up with the excuses anymore."

"There's no social studies project," said Simon, looking like he might cry. "You have to help me!"

"Psst. Aly."

Aly decided to stop pretending and opened her eyes. Faking it until she fell asleep just wasn't going to cut it—not in Rachael's room. Even if her sleeping bag on the floor was comfortable—and it wasn't—her big sister's favorite thing to collect was scented candles, and Aly felt overwhelmed by all the intense smells around her: Christmas peppermint and Halloween cinnamon and made-up scents like Restful Morning and Honolulu Sunrise.

And behind all of it, the faint scent of burning paper.

Those memories weren't exactly helping her sleep, either.

"*Als.*"

Aly sighed. "*What?*" she whispered.

Rachael shifted on her bed and faced her. Aly could vaguely see her sister's eyes glimmer in the pulsing light from her charging computer.

"Dude, what *happened*?" asked Rachael.

"I have no idea," Aly admitted.

"Do you think it's the same thing that happened at school?"

"I don't know," Aly replied, not sure why her sister was asking that. Of course it felt sketchy that she'd dealt with sudden, unexplained fires twice in one day. But how was she supposed to explain it? What was Rachael getting at?

"But did it *feel* the same?" asked Rachael. "Like, when you saw the fire, was it—"

"I don't know, Rach, okay?" Aly sat up and faced her sister.

She sensed it then, only for an instant. In the way Rachael shrank back into her blankets, in the way those eyes gleamed a little brighter and wider, in the silence that hung in the wake of her outburst.

Fear. Rachael was afraid of her. Rachael, Aly's

older sister, who had once walked in front of a moving car to retrieve a dropped doll. Who had put Jess in her place earlier that afternoon without blinking an eye. Who was popular and pretty and could argue her way out of anything, anytime.

She was scared of her. Aly, the quiet sister. The one who was supposed to always be there for the other two.

"Sorry," said Aly. "I just . . . had a long day." Aly lay awkwardly down and closed her eyes.

When she finally got to sleep, she dreamed that she was sitting on a beach of black sand with flames rolling across the surface of the ocean as far as the eye could see.

WHERE THERE'S
SMOKE . . .

"You cool, hon?"

It took Aly a second to realize that Mom was talking to her. Aly glanced next to her, only to discover that her brother and sister had already left the car; Simon stood at the open door, waiting for her to disembark. When she looked up, she saw Mom's eyes in the rearview mirror, full of worry.

"I'm cool, Mom," returned Aly with a sharp nod. She didn't want to freak Mom out, especially with everything that had happened over the course of the last twenty-four hours.

"You know you can talk to me about all this, right?" Mom pressed.

"I know." Aly unbuckled her seat belt and grabbed her backpack. She did, too—Mom was a middle child like her, all support, all emotions (at least until she was a teenager, when she'd apparently gone all black and spikes, but even that felt like a big heart move). *I'm cool* was what Mom called "the middle child mantra," letting other middles know you're okay while dealing with everyone else's problems.

This time around, though, Aly wasn't sure she wanted more focus on her problems, from Mom or anyone else. Between Rachael's room smelling like candy and the bad dreams, she'd slept terribly and was more tired than she'd ever been. She just wanted to get through the day, go home, and go straight to bed without thinking about fire.

As they walked up the path toward school, Simon

talked about how he and his friend Andrew were still worried about Bentley Moss tormenting them, but Aly was barely listening. Her shoulders ached under her backpack, and her fatigue made the whole world feel dull and muffled around her. When they got inside, she gave Simon a quick hug and marched off to class with all the grace and emotions of a robot.

Math class seemed to happen around her—everyone filing in and taking their seats, Ms. Valez coming in and starting the lesson. The only things her mind seemed to be able to focus on were memories from the previous day, of fire rising out of nowhere, destroying her room, blazing so close and so hot that she'd noticed some of her right eyebrow missing that night as she brushed her teeth.

That, and frightened faces. Ray in the lab, looking tiny and confused. Rachael and Simon inside her bedroom, her dumbstruck, him horrified. Rachael's face in the dark, pulling away from Aly, mouth clapping shut, as though scared of saying the wrong thing and making her angry—

"Ms. Theland?"

Aly snapped back to reality. Ms. Valez stood at her desk, one fist planted against one round hip. She looked down at Aly with bored impatience.

"Yes?" asked Aly.

"The assignment, Ms. Theland?" asked Ms. Valez with a sigh. "Your homework? I assume you *did* the assignment?"

Aly blurted the truth before she could stop herself. "Mine caught on fire."

The whole class laughed at once around her; she could hear Jess two rows back mumble, "*Such* a loser."

Aly lowered her head and hunched her shoulders.

Ms. Valez rolled her eyes. "Ms. Theland, I heard about your incident yesterday, but we can't just get out of *every* class with *I set it on fire.*"

The classroom laughed even louder. Part of Aly wished she could shrink down into her clothes like a turtle, hide herself forever . . .

But another part of her *burned*.

No matter what had happened over the past couple of days, Ms. Valez was a bully. She always had been, interrupting the quiet kids by telling them to speak up, reading passed notes aloud in class. Aly had gotten by on being unnoticeable, but now she was apparently in the spotlight.

Well, Ms. Valez, she thought, *you picked the wrong day to notice me.*

She pulled her backpack from under her desk, fished around in it until she found the note her mom had written, and shoved it so hard under Ms. Valez's nose that the math teacher took a step back.

"Here, if you don't believe me," Aly snapped.

Ms. Valez took the note and unfolded it like she was worried it had a live snake inside. She read Mom's explanation, nodded swiftly, and mumbled something about Aly making sure she had her homework the next day before moving on.

"Hey, Theland." Aly glanced up and caught the eyes of Kieren Jiu, who sat in front of her. The boy had twisted around to look back, and gave her a smirk and thumbs-up. "Way to call Valez out. What a jerk, right?"

Aly smiled and nodded before looking back down at her desk. For once, she didn't feel like her break in invisibility was a bad thing. Maybe snapping at Ms. Valez wasn't exactly the most levelheaded thing to do, but she knew deep down that it was right. Who told that woman it was okay to pick on people?

It wasn't Aly's usual way. But she was warming up to it.

Rachael checked in on her right after first period. She stood like a prison guard, facing Aly but scanning the hallways in her bejeweled sunglasses, staring down anyone who looked at them.

"I'm fine, Rachael," she said. "I'm just heading to the bathroom between classes. No one's gonna mess with me."

"Okay, well . . . don't take any attitude from these jerks," Rachael replied.

"I'm not going to get any *attitude*," groaned Aly before heading into the bathroom.

She was washing her hands when Jess snapped a finger in her face.

The sudden noise and motion caught Aly off guard, and she stumbled back, her shoulder blades colliding uncomfortably with the green tile wall. Jess stood with her backpack dangling from one hand like some kind of mace, an ugly little smile pulled across her mouth. Behind her, Kristy and Athena watched the door, looking both worried and excited.

"Your sister isn't here to stand up for you this time," said Jess.

Run was the first instinct that flashed across Aly's mind, making her heart thud in her chest and the blood pound in her ears. She'd never been in a fight, and Jess's posture told her that she was hoping for one. It wouldn't be too out of sorts for her—Jess's own older sister, Grace, was known for taking a swing at anyone who bothered her. But even if Aly did get past her old friend, Athena and Kristy probably wouldn't let her leave.

She was cornered.

Jess lunged, raising her backpack. Aly cringed away and made a soft noise in her throat.

"God, *look* at you." Jess laughed, lowering her bag and shaking her head. "Aly, you're so *sad*. Did you really think for a second I was going to hit you? I *know* you. I *know* how weak you are. Besides, I might cut my knuckles on all that horrible metal crap in your mouth."

Fear, embarrassment, and helplessness clouded Aly's mind . . . but beneath it all, there was something else. Something she wasn't familiar with, something that she could feel growing and searing the walls of her brain.

Hatred. She hated Jess. For making her flinch. For making fun of her braces. But most of all, for becoming this person who now stood before her. She hated how betrayed she felt by this girl who used to be her best friend. She hated Jess so much, she thought it might give her a nosebleed.

"You know, I was wrong to call you a pyro yesterday," said Jess, shrugging on her backpack. "That'd mean you liked fire . . . and there's nothing *hot* about you, Jess. You're cold."

"Jess," said Kristy.

"Like a fish." Jess laughed. "Or some kind of lizard—"

"Jess, your backpack is smoking!" cried Kristy, pointing.

"What?" Jess twisted to look over her shoulder. Aly could see that Kristy was right—thick gray curls of smoke were coming off Jess's backpack, growing bigger, smelling harsh and acrid, and—

Jess's backpack went up in a blast of flames. "What— No!" screamed Jess, frantically slapping at it, and then suddenly the flames were on the straps, singeing the ends of her hair, licking at her scrunchie. Jess tugged frantically at her straps, but her violent movements only tangled her further in the flaming nylon.

"I'm burning!" screamed Jess. *"I'm burning!"* She dropped to her back and began to roll around the room, but the flames didn't go away. If anything, the fire only got bigger as she rolled, as if there was lighter fluid on the bathroom floor, and soon Jess wasn't yelling words, just screaming, shrieking guttural gibberish syllables as she frantically tried to suffocate the flames. The sound frightened Aly, made her feel nauseous . . . and yet she couldn't look away.

"What is going on in here?" screamed Ms. Valez, barging into the smoke-filled bathroom. The door flying open brought Aly out of her trance, and she barreled past Ms. Valez and out into the hall, pushing her way past students and faculty rushing toward the smoking bathroom doorway.

Jess's screams followed her down the hall.

HOT TAKE

The school library felt like the safest bet for an escape. Aly stormed in so fast that Ms. Berrera looked up from where she was reading *A Wrinkle in Time* to some of the lower schoolers. Aly did her best to wave and smile normally, then fled to the back of the shelves. She found a corner, crouched down among all the old, sour-smelling books, and put her face in her hands.

What. Happened?

It couldn't be. She couldn't *hate someone on fire*.

And yet for the third time in two days, it felt like Aly's bad mood had caused a blaze.

Not only that, but the more she thought about it, the more Aly realized each fire had felt different but appropriate. With Ray, she wanted to scare her lab partner, so she lit up the table. With her homework, she'd become frustrated, and the whole desk burned up. And now she'd been angry at a specific person—and that person had caught on fire.

It didn't just feel like the fire started *when* she was angry. It felt like the fire *was* her anger.

She forced herself to breathe a little slower. The image of Jess rolling around on the floor with that terrified, open-mouthed look on her face kept playing on repeat in her mind, but bit by bit, she forced it out and concentrated on calming down. Panicking wasn't helping. She needed to do what she always did, and think this through.

So . . .

Let's say I'm setting people on fire with my mind, she thought.

That's ridiculous.

And it was. She wasn't some little kid. She knew that.

But it sure seemed like that was what was happening.

There was a name for that, she knew. She couldn't remember it, but starting fires . . . making fires happen . . . she'd heard about it, or seen it on TV. Did one of the Avengers do that? She couldn't remember.

Carefully, Aly stood up, brushed herself down, and headed to one of the computers in the library.

Starting fires got her a bunch of links about crisis hotlines and what to do when your dysfunctional children were committing arson. *Fire mind power* didn't help much, either, and gave her a bunch of images of comic-book heroes. Nothing she found had any practical information—

Wait. There.

Aly froze on the Wiki link. She read the word and rolled it softly around in her mouth.

Pyrokinesis. Pie. Roh. Kuh. Knee. Sis.

She clicked through and began scanning the details. Pyrokinesis, the psychic ability to create, control, or predict fires. Possibilities for destruction: endless. Mostly used as sort of a magic trick back in the nineteenth century, but reports of a girl in the Philippines being able to do it in 2011 were also there. Also common: the context of *fire ghosts*—spirits who were killed by fire and could now start them after—

Aly sat back from the computer and put a hand to her forehead. Was she really doing this? Reading about *fire ghosts* like they were real?

There had to be a rational explanation. She just needed everything to slow down so she could get her head straight.

"Hey, Theland?"

Fear lurched in Aly. She closed the browser window as quickly as she could, then looked up to see Kieren Jiu—only this time, the boy didn't smile or shoot her a thumbs-up. This time, he looked worried and flustered, and there was a quiver in his voice. Aly wondered if he'd heard about Jess, and she felt cold.

"What's up?" asked Aly,

"Your brother's Simon, right?" asked Kieren.

"Yes," she said.

"He's about to get the crap beaten out of him."

Aly didn't wait for further explanation—she got up, Kieren pointed, and she ran in that direction.

She hit the bars to the cafeteria's double doors with full speed. Kids flew back as she burst in, and Aly mumbled feeble apologies as her eyes scanned the room.

"I'm talking to you, idiot!"

The scene made Aly want to cry. Simon stood there, his head hung, staring at his lunch tray on the floor. His fish sticks, tater tots, and peas lay strewn about his feet. Bentley Moss loomed over Simon, jamming a finger in his face.

"Now it's *all* on the floor," snapped Moss. "You happy?"

"HEY!" Aly ran out in front of Simon before she knew what she was thinking. "You leave him alone!"

"Tss," said Moss with a sneer. "Little whiner needs big sis to save the day."

"What's your problem?" said Aly. She did her best to sound angry, but in truth, she could feel herself shaking with fear. This wasn't her way—breaking up fights, yelling at people in front of the whole school. And truthfully, up close, she understood why Simon was so scared of this kid. He was only a year older than Simon, but an early bloomer, taller and rangier than the other boys in his class. *If he hits me*, she thought, *it's going to hurt.*

"Your brother dropped a ketchupy tot on my new kicks," snapped Bentley, pointing to the thin red smear on one of his massive white high-tops. "I stay up all night to get these shoes online, I wait three weeks for them, and that little idiot ruins them in an *instant*."

"They're *shoes*, man," said Aly. "You're going to pick on someone for *shoes*?"

"They're *limited edition*," said Moss.

"Oh, I'm sorry if my brother is gonna make you look bad on the sneakerhead Reddit," said Aly. Around her, the onlookers rumbled with laughter. *It felt good*, she thought, and turned some of her cold panic into hot anger. She could see by his clenched brow and pursed-up mouth that Bentley felt it, too. "This is a stupid thing to act like a bully about. Leave my brother alone."

"Tss," said Moss. He flicked his fingers in Aly's face, like he was shooing a dog. "Or what, big sis? Or *what*?"

44

The gesture made Aly's anger bloom white and fiery inside her. It was like Ray slapping her hand away—the ultimate sign of disrespect. She wasn't taking that anymore.

Her eyes went down to Moss's feet, to the bulky white-and-purple kicks he'd humiliated her brother over.

Could she?

She focused on them and pushed her anger. Pointed it. Pressed it all into a single burning dot . . .

"Hey!" snapped Moss. "I *said*—"

He took a step forward—and slid.

A high-pitched squeak of sneaker on linoleum ripped through the cafeteria, and all eyes were on Bentley Moss as he tried to regain balance. But everywhere he put his foot, he slid—and left behind him a streak of steaming rubber.

"What—*yo*, what's happening?" cried Moss. An especially hard slip sent him tumbling to the floor. The kids in the cafeteria burst into more laughter . . . but it quickly turned to gasps as the soles of Bentley Moss's shoes began to melt before their eyes, bubbling and dripping in thick strings of white rubber all over Simon's fallen tots. Acrid blue smoke rose from the gooey mess. Immediately, the onlooking crowd became a ring of phones filming the bizarre event.

Aly felt the smile grow on her face as her eyes focused on the melting shoes. She knew she shouldn't stay long, that it might give her away if she was filmed watching Moss's shoes melt so intently.

Small, familiar hands grasped at her arms from behind.

"What's going on?" cried Simon. "Why are his shoes doing that?"

"He'll be fine," said Aly. She tried to shield her brother from the sight, not wanting to scare him, and yet she couldn't stop looking at the bubbling mess of the bully's shoes, even as Simon began to drag her away.

BURNT OFFERING

There it was. She could see Mom through the driver's-side window. It was now or never.

Aly power walked out the doors of school and across the school lawn to the family car out front. The hundred feet she had to navigate might as well have been a hundred miles. And along the way, there were land mines.

She felt the stares and whispers more than she

saw or heard them. All around her, kids from every grade paused what they were doing and observed Aly Theland. They wondered aloud about the things they'd heard, the stuff they'd seen that day. Smoke pouring out of the second-floor girls' bathroom. Jess Gregor's backpack outside the nurse's office, a blackened hunk. The janitor had to use something special to get Bentley Moss's shoe goo off the cafeteria floor. And then there was Ray Westra yesterday . . .

Something's up with that girl, they whispered. *Something's wrong with her.*

Danger: flammable, she thought, and hung her head.

"I'm cool," she said as she got to the car, before Mom could ask.

"That boy is staring at you," whispered Mom. "The one with the track jacket. He's cute!"

"Mom!" whispered Aly, and then climbed into the back of the car mumbling, "I'm fine. It's fine. Everything's fine. I just want to go home."

She plopped silently down next to Simon and Rachael, glanced at them, and could tell she wasn't very convincing. Her brother and sister stared at her like she had grown fangs. At her eye contact, they quickly looked away and pretended to be interested in the car's upholstery, but Aly had seen it.

"So, anything fun happen at school today?" asked Mom as they pulled out onto the street. "Rachael, when are they voting for queen of the April Showers Dance? Think you're still in the running?"

"You know, actually, Mom, I think I'm over it," said Rachael with a sigh, staring out the window.

"Wow, just like that?" Mom laughed. "You were obsessed a week ago!"

Rachael shrugged and smiled. "I know. But honestly? It all seems kind of shallow now. It's just a popularity contest. Why should I care? There are more important things out there."

"Good for you, sweetie!" said Mom. "Simon, Aly, consider this your sister being a good example."

"Well, let's not go too far," mumbled Rachael.

It's easy for her, thought Aly. *She gets to choose to be something. I don't get any choice. I'm a freak by nature.* She rubbed her eyes and tried to watch the scenery pass, but kept imagining every tree engulfed in flames.

Her homework was done in a blur. If there was one thing Aly knew from all her time staying the course and holding down the fort, it was that the easiest way to draw attention to yourself was to break protocol. In school, that meant showing up with her homework not done. Two or three days like that, and she'd end up having a heart-to-heart with Mr. Kunhalder, the guidance counselor. So what if most of her answers were iffy—as long as it was a B-minus or better, she'd survive. Teachers didn't really care; they just wanted it done.

And when her homework was done, she read everything she could find online about pyrokinesis.

It wasn't much—a lot of comic-book characters again, a lot of poorly designed paranormal investigation shows on YouTube, one horror movie after another—but one or two pages gave her a gold mine of material. Apparently, it was just one of many mental powers people could have. There was good ol' telekinesis, moving something with your mind; telepathy, reading minds and talking with your mind; hydrokinesis, controlling water; technokinesis, controlling technology and machinery; somnokinesis, controlling dreams; and ectokinesis, controlling ghosts or the soul. (The last two creeped Aly out—she hoped she'd never meet someone who could mess with her dreams.)

The information about pyrokinesis pointed in all different directions. One site said you had to be born under a fire sign during a solar flare. Others said it was all brain chemistry.

There was only one theme Aly encountered in everything she read:

Destruction.

Almost every rumored account of pyrokinesis she found online included homes going up in flames and people dying. Farms were razed overnight. Schools and churches were turned to ash in a matter of hours. In one story, a seaside town's lighthouse somehow burned down during a heavy rainstorm; everywhere else flooded, according to the news report, but the lighthouse burned so hot the gears inside melted. The suspected pyrokinetic was found in the wreckage, unharmed.

This is me, she thought to herself, speechless.

Me, Aly Theland. I put muffins in the oven, keep my head down at school . . . and I'm an agent of pure chaos.

"It is you, isn't it?"

Aly's heart leaped in her throat. She looked to the door of her room and found Rachael leaning against the frame, eyeing her.

"What?" she asked.

"It's you setting the fires," said Rachael. "But . . . doing it special, somehow. Like with your mind, maybe, or—or your *stare*, or something."

Boom.

Just like that, Aly felt helpless, pinned to the spot, caught red-handed.

Could Rachael see her screen? No—no, that'd be too easy.

Somehow, her sister just knew.

How could she not? She'd probably seen Aly standing there, eyeing Bentley Moss's sneakers as they melted for all the world to see.

The middle child in her told her to keep quiet. To make up something ridiculous and continue doing research on her own. But the sibling in her knew that trying to lie to Rachael was like struggling against quicksand. And another part, the new part, the part that drove her to stand between her brother and a bully—that part told her to let it out.

"I think so," Aly said.

"I knew it!" Rachael stepped in and closed the bedroom door behind her. "I can't believe this. I thought you were going to say I was out of my mind."

Aly tried to say something—but suddenly, she felt so heavy with it all. The last two days of stress, fear, confusion, and blasting heat seemed to land on her shoulders at once. Before she knew what was happening, she started breathing fast and felt her eyes sting. The room swam around her, and she hunched forward and put her face in her hands.

"Whoa, I'm sorry, I didn't mean anything by that." Rachael moved beside Aly and put a hand on her shoulder. "It's okay, Als. It's not like you hurt anyone. I mean, Jess's hair is going to be a little punk rock for a while, but I heard she wasn't burned all that much."

"I just feel so . . . out of control," croaked Aly. "Like, what if I get angry and really hurt someone? What if I burn the house down, and we don't have time to get out, and you or Mom or Dad or *Simon*—"

"Hey. Look at me." Rachael crouched to get on Aly's level and looked her hard in the eyes. "You are not going to do that. We're going to figure this out, and we're going to be fine. I'm always going to be here with you."

Aly nodded. She felt her breathing slow down, and the world around her seemed to settle into place. "Thanks, Rachael. Sorry, I'm a *mess* right now."

"Of course you are," said Rachael. "You just found out you can start fires with your brain. This is *big*, sister. It's going to take time. But first things first: What have you found out on your own?"

"What do you mean?" asked Aly.

"Have you tried your powers yet?" asked Rachael, knitting her hands. "Have you taken yourself for a test run?"

"No—nothing like that," said Aly. "I'm too scared that I'll mess up and someone will burn alive. Just Internet research. I mean, this one page says—"

"Aly, people on the Internet think the earth is flat and that you can secretly eat detergent pods. Any idiot can write anything on there. But, so, you've never tried it. You know . . . using your powers to make something happen."

"No," said Aly. Then again, the more she thought about it, she realized that wasn't true. "Well . . . Bentley Moss's sneakers. I tried, that time. And it worked. But I didn't feel in control. And I'm scared— scared that if I'm not in control . . ."

"And it's totally okay to feel that way," said Rachael. "I'm not trying to force you to do anything. But with something this monumental, it might be time to *take* control."

"I'm listening," said Aly.

FIRE DRILL

In the corner of her eye, Aly saw Simon make a weird face when Rachael mentioned a "special sisters hike" the next day, but Dad seemed to believe the lie. From where she listened in the next room, Aly was surprised by just how good at lying her sister had become. All the lines were exactly what they'd rehearsed, down to Rachael whispering, "I think she's having some problems at school right now. She might need girl time." She was totally believable.

The woods at the end of their street were patchy and a little trash strewn, but Aly knew from previous walks there with the family that they were also deep and private. The sisters took the main gravel path a ways, and then turned off between the trees, to the jutting boulder that she and Rachael used to call their "castle peak" as children, perfect for playing princess on.

"This should be good," said Rachael. She set down her backpack and pulled out a mini fire extinguisher, a box of barbecue matches, and some paper. Gratitude warmed Aly from the inside—her sister might be bossy, dramatic, and way too worried about what other people thought of her, but she was also *prepared*. Aly was so busy trying to either tamp down her emotions or make sense of them that she hadn't thought to bring anything, but Rachael had done the planning for her.

"How do we even begin?" Aly asked.

"I think we start easy." Rachael retrieved one of the long wooden barbecue matches from its box and handed it to Aly. "Light the match."

Aly sat on the rock, held out the match, and concentrated on the chalky red dot of the head.

Light, she thought. She squinted hard.

Burst into flames.

Catch on fire.

"This feels ridiculous," she said. "All I can think about is how we use these matches to light pumpkins at Halloween."

"Dude, stop sabotaging yourself," groaned Rachael. "If you think it's silly, it'll never happen. *Believe. Be* the fire."

"All I am is some girl sitting on a rock staring at a match."

"Will you just—*here.*" Rachael fluttered around Aly and helped her cross her legs, sit up straight, hold her head up high. She swiped hair out of Aly's face and then crouched in front of her with her hands out. "Okay, breathe deep. Clear your mind of thought. Focus only on the power. And then direct it at the match. Envision it lighting."

Aly nodded absently. She inhaled through her nose, exhaled out her mouth. She blinked slow and let her mind drain of all thought. She focused on her breathing, on the sounds around her, on the stillness of her body. Her eyes locked on the head of the match, imagining the sharp hiss of its igniting, the smell of the sulfur, the flash of the head, the flicker of the flame, and . . .

And . . .

She huffed and dropped the match. "Nope. Nothing. That was very relaxing, but it didn't feel like the power."

"No, come on, Als, *nothing* isn't acceptable," said Rachael. "If you want to control this, you've got to work at it. Think about your breath. Focus your mind the way you did earlier, with Jess and with Bentley—"

"Yeah, except I *wasn't* focused then, Rachael," snapped Aly, running her hands through her hair. "It was the opposite, I was *furious*. If anything, I wasn't thinking at all. I was just *feeling*."

When she looked back at Rachael, her older sister was rubbing her chin and nodding to herself. But it was the look on her face—the look that Aly had seen before in her life, when Rachael decided that something crazy was the answer to everyone's problems—that made her worry.

"Rachael, what are you thinking?" Aly asked.

"Well . . . okay," said Rachael. "Just bear with me for a second."

SNAP!

The tip of Aly's nose exploded in pain. She cried out and covered her nose, but Rachael flicked her again, harder, between the eyes.

"What's wrong with you?" she yelped at her sister.

"Aw, does little Aly not like it when someone gives her a little flick?" said Rachael in a baby-talk voice.

The truth came over Aly, and she rolled her eyes. "Nice try, Rachael. It'll take a lot more than a few flicks in the face to make me really angry."

Rachael looked frustrated . . . and then a smile stretched out across her face. It was a smile Aly had seen on Rachael as a child, shortly before Aly was talked out of the toy she was holding or the ice cream she was eating. A face Aly didn't like.

"Yeah, because Aly's got her impenetrable shield up, right?" said Rachael. "No one can get to Aly. Helping out around the house and getting her brother dressed and never once feeling upset or bitter about it. Because she's so perfect. Such a saint."

"I get it," said Aly. "You're a real master of psychology, Rach—"

"You know what your little mantra with Mom means, right?" said Rachael. "You can act like it's some middle-child solidarity, but we all know what *you're cool* means, right? It means, *I don't have time for you, Aly.* It means, *As long as you're* cool, *then you can just stay invisible a little longer while I focus on what's actually important.*"

Aly tried to speak, to laugh at Rachael's attempt to rile her up, but all she could do was open and close her mouth a few times. She hadn't expected this—Rachael going so deep, getting so . . . personal with her feelings. It made her feel uncomfortable, unprepared, shoved into the spotlight. Because, worst of all, it was like Rachael had somehow read her mind. That thought had always bothered her, had always nagged at the back of her mind. And somehow, Rachael had known.

"Let's go back," said Aly, returning the matches to Rachael's bag.

"And Aly's nice enough to play along, too," cooed Rachael. "Oh yeah, if you need someone to be not a problem, to just sit there and *take it*, then Aly Theland's your girl. No one romantically interested. No friends except the one who ditched her for cooler friends. Just Aly with her mouth full of braces and her head down."

Aly kept her back to her sister and frantically shoved the rest of the things in the backpack. It was here again—the pressure from within, like the feelings in her heart were pressing against her brain. The feeling that made her want to scream and kick over a table, the swelling explosion that had blanked out her mind when she'd melted Bentley Moss's shoes. She could feel the muscles in her face giving it away, dragging her mouth down in a miserable scowl. She wouldn't give Rachael the satisfaction of seeing it.

"Aly thinks she's so much better than everyone, because she takes care of everyone, but we all know the truth," said Rachael.

"I don't think I'm better than anyone," grumbled Aly.

"And that's that everyone *pities* her. They eat her muffins and pat her head and make sure she's so *cool*, because it's hard being as much of a *nobody* as Aly is."

It was too much. She spun and faced Rachael, hot tears stinging the edges of her eyes.

"Shut up, Rachael, that's not true."

"Because we all know Aly *is* nothing, and *will be* nothing," Rachael persisted.

"Shut your mouth!" snapped Aly.

"And once Simon can dress himself and Mom and Dad retire, there'll just be boring little Aly there, collecting cats and making meals no one wants and leaving us all to wonder what to do with someone who was never important enough to matter—"

Aly gritted her teeth, clenched her fists . . .

And then the scream ripped out of her. The one she'd been holding in for years, the one that'd been shattering every window in the church of her heart for as long as she could remember. She screamed as loud and as hard as anyone she'd ever known.

The oak directly behind Rachael erupted in fire.

The blast was so huge and hot that Rachael fell to the ground and Aly had to shield her face. The tree wasn't burning so much as it was *on fire*, with huge columns of almost-white flame blasting out of it on all sides, belching a column of smoke that cut the evening sky in half.

Aly fell to her knees and watched it burn. The flames running up the tree were beautiful to her, like water in reverse. Like her feelings were finally made whole and let out into the world.

In an instant, it was over—Rachael ran over with the extinguisher and began spraying the oak with white foaming liquid. Though the whole tree had been burning, a few sprays seemed to do the trick, with Rachael targeting all the right spots to douse the blaze.

With the last flame extinguished, Aly felt the heat of the moment leave her as though it had evaporated. She hugged her arms to herself as she stared at the blackened surface of the oak tree, watched fireproof foam leak down its trunk, like her own despair in the wake of her anger. Before, at the prospect of having this new ability, she'd actually started considering what she could *do* with it . . . and now she was learning the horrible truth of the matter.

"Well," said Rachael, jogging back over to her, "the good news is, it's definitely you. And it's your anger that's causing it."

And the bad news, thought Aly, *is that I can't control it.*

FIREPROOF

Over the years, Aly had gotten pretty used to putting on a brave face and acting like she didn't have a care in the world. A big part of keeping her head down without a lot of problems was looking and sounding totally nondescript during family dinners; Mom was a born worrier about the people she loved, just like Aly, and Dad liked to butt in with lousy advice because, well, he was a dad. So even when something was really bugging Aly, she managed to make it look like everything was okay. Smile, eat a vegetable, maybe direct the conversation to somebody else.

Tonight, it wasn't so simple. As Aly forked her chicken and Israeli couscous around her plate, all she could see was a never-ending loop of the moment the oak tree caught fire, the way the flames blasted out and rode up the trunk like water in reverse. She felt the heat slicing across her face, smelled the sudden mix of ozone and wood smoke . . . and heard the things Rachael had said to set her off.

Everyone pities her . . . because it's hard being as much of a nobody as Aly is.

Her eyes flickered to Dad, then Mom, then Simon. Was that it? Did everything she did for the family just make them feel sorry for her? No, it couldn't be. They loved her, they appreciated her. It was just . . .

No one romantically interested. No friends except the one who ditched her for cooler friends. Just Aly with her mouth full of braces and her head down.

She closed her eyes hard as she felt the sting of those insults again. Because where was the lie? Did she have any life to speak of? She'd lost Jess to friends who people actually cared about, even if they were stupid, shallow ones. No one had even come close to asking her to the April Showers Dance; she'd never even heard a rumor that anyone thought she was cute. Somehow, by trying to get by without making waves, she'd built a life that no one cared about—

"Aly?"

Her eyes popped open. Across the table, Mom shot her a concerned smile.

"What?" Aly asked.

"You cool, kiddo?"

We all know what you're cool *means, right? It means,* I don't have time for you. *It means,* Just stay invisible a little longer.

"Why do you keep asking that?" Aly asked her mother. Maybe a little too fast. Maybe a little too loud.

Mom reared her head back and blinked a few times. "Oh, just . . . you know," she said with a soft laugh. "The middle child mantra, right?"

"I mean, I'm more than just a middle child, though," Aly pressed. The pain from Rachael's comments earlier seemed to crackle inside her. "My whole life isn't just whether I'm *cool* or not."

Hurt flashed across Mom's face, but she nodded

hard. "Of course, honey, you're right." The gesture only set Aly's anger off more—Mom pulling an Aly, swallowing her feelings and trying to go along, get along. Aly had to have learned it from somewhere, right? And now she could feel everyone else at the table looking at her, judging her, wondering *what was wrong with her*—

She caught movement from the corner of her eye. Rachael was staring at her gravely, and was drawing her hand up and down around her chest. Aly recognized the motion: *Deep breaths. In. Out.* She realized that her feelings must be written all over her face.

And Rachael had seen firsthand what might happen if Aly got too angry.

"Sorry," she grumbled, looking down at her plate. "It's fine. I must be tired. Rachael and I went on a long hike today."

After dinner, she offered to clear the table, and Simon helped. She could sense him going the distance, carrying too-heavy serving dishes and loading the dishwasher.

"You don't need to help me," said Aly. "I can handle it myself."

"I know," said Simon from the sink. "I just felt like helping."

"Yeah, well . . . it's fine if you just want to do your own thing," she said. "You don't need to humor me."

When her little brother didn't respond, she assumed he'd taken her advice. But then she heard his voice, small and hoarse, behind her.

"Thanks, Aly," he said. "Thanks for everything you do for us."

His tone made her turn to him. Simon stood in the middle of the room, kneading his hands in front of him. In his face, Aly saw every emotion she'd never wish on him—shame, confusion, guilt . . .

And don't forget fear, she thought. It was true. Just like Rachael that night in her room, Simon was frightened of her. Whether it was what he'd seen her do earlier, or the way she'd lashed out at their mom during dinner, she couldn't tell. But she'd made him scared of her.

"Simon," she said, and took a step forward.

Simon flinched back toward the door.

Aly's heart hurt, and her throat swelled. She nodded to herself, said, "Sorry," and turned back to the dishes. When she next turned around, Simon was gone.

She was on her way upstairs when she heard Dad say her name from behind her parents' bedroom door. She stopped, took a step back, and listened.

"I'll talk to her about it tomorrow," said Dad's voice.

"No, don't," said Mom's. "That's the last thing she needs. She shows individuality one time, and suddenly we're having little talks with her about it?" She sighed. "It was on me this time. I can't just expect her to be my pal all her life. She's almost a teenager. I just . . ." Her voice cracked with tears. "I just wish she could tell me what she's going through. The troubles at school, her burned room . . . I just wish I could know . . ."

"Aw, honey."

Aly could picture the scene now. Dad coming over and holding Mom. Mom crying and waving him away, but letting him stay there.

Both of them wondering what they were going to do about her.

She went to Rachael's room and closed the door. She tried to lock it, then remembered that Rachael's twelfth birthday present had been a key lock on her bedroom door.

"I can lock it if you need me to," said Rachael, looking up from scribbling in her diary.

"It doesn't matter," said Aly, facing her sister with a sigh. "Point is, we need to figure this out."

Rachael blinked a few times. "What do you mean? More research?"

"Yeah, but not field research." Aly marched over and hopped up onto Rachael's bed. The sugary smell of scented candles made her want to gag, but she forced herself to focus on the task at hand. "Now that we know that I *am* doing this, we need to change our tactics."

"Shoes off," said Rachael, flapping her fingers at Aly. "What are you thinking? I've looked into the idea of curing it, but there's nothing. Usually, people grow out of it. This might take time."

Aly yanked off her shoes and looked hard at her sister. "You saw me get angry at dinner tonight."

Rachael closed her diary. "Yeah. You scared the living daylights out of me, Als."

"Exactly. I'm not going to stop being this thing. And, if we're being honest . . ." Aly took a deep breath and let it out hard. "I'm not going to stop being angry. Now that I'm letting it out here and there, I think it's going to keep coming out. Maybe I've been angry for a long time now. Maybe I have some pent-up emotions. But as long as my anger is causing these problems, I need to know how to keep it in check."

"No offense, but I'm not surprised," said Rachael. "Also, seventh grade is rough. You're totally allowed to be angry, Als. But you're also right that we can't let anyone get hurt. Especially our family." She sighed and clapped her hands. "Okay, so what's step one? Where do we begin?"

"Breathing exercises?" asked Aly.

"Sounds like an easy Google search," said Rachael. "Baby steps. Let's do it."

CONTROLLED BLAZE

As she stepped out of the car, Aly took an eight-second breath in, held it for two seconds, and let it out for four. She held her head high and felt the sun on her face. She thanked the universe for giving her a beautiful spring morning like this one. She saw the beauty in all things.

"Aly?" said Simon. "I can't get out with you standing there."

She moved so Simon could get out of the car.

"How're you feeling?" Rachael asked, walking backward in front of her as they headed down the path to school. This was one of their tactics—Rachael keeping eye contact, distracting Aly from everyone around her whispering and pointing. Rachael waved to a friend here and there, but otherwise focused solely on Aly.

"Really good," said Aly, shooting her a genuine smile. It *had* been a great morning, both by Aly standards and not-burning-the-house-down standards. She'd made everyone toast, helped Simon pack his bag, and had given Mom a big hug on the way out the door. It was only day one, but it looked like the rules she and Rachael had come up with the night before were working.

There were four main points they'd discussed that Aly wanted to hit every time. The first three were breath, treats, and gratitude. She had to breathe slowly and carefully, making sure to keep her pulse steady and her head clear. She had to enjoy little moments of sensation—things she saw and thought were cute, songs she loved, even good smells—and let them radiate joy in her life. And finally, she had to take a moment to count her blessings whenever she could and show gratitude for them.

Most important, though, was what Rachael called *letting it flow.* "Your anger is like a river, you know?" she'd said. "If you put up a dam, it's going to back up until we have this big lake of Aly anger. You have to be open about when you're not happy. Don't hold it in, just let it flow. Be honest with yourself."

For now, at least, Aly felt like she was flowing. She noticed a boy from the sixth grade pointing at her and whispering, and her frustration came . . . and went.

"I gotta peel off," said Rachael, motioning toward the door. "You're gonna be okay, right?"

"I think so," said Aly. "Thanks, Rachael."

"You need me for any reason, you text me." Rachael passed through the door, turned, and hustled off to where her friend Lauren was waiting for her. The frizzy-haired girl waved to Rachael, but shot Aly the firm, awkward nod of *We don't really know each other, and from what I've heard lately, that's fine.*

Blocking out the chatter around her wasn't entirely possible, but Aly did her best to ignore all distractions on the way to class. Mostly what she heard was her own name—*Aly Theland, Aly Theland*, whispered again and again around her. But she breathed, and stopped at a water fountain for a cool drink, and thanked the universe for how light her history workbook was, and suddenly the sound of her name didn't matter so much.

This could work, she thought to herself. *It's not exactly a long-term solution, but it could—*

A shoulder collided with hers, throttling her out of her head. She spun to see Grover Berchette, a boy from Rachael's class, tall and gangly. He looked up from his phone with an annoyed face—but when he saw Aly, he blanched.

"Sorry," he said, holding up a palm. "Didn't see you. Totally my bad."

"It's fine. I need to watch where I'm going," said Aly, letting it flow.

She watched him turn and jog down the halls. A few feet away, his friends all stared at him with similarly shaken faces.

It's because of me, she thought. *They've heard the stories. They're worried.*

She breathed. She shrugged her shoulders a little—felt all right. She was grateful for the boy's apology, frightened though it was.

She let it flow.

See? she thought. *You can do this. They might be scared, but who cares? You are strong, Aly. You have the power here.*

In English, she answered a question about *A Midsummer Night's Dream* and didn't get upset when Vivian Meyer's Arizona Iced Tea fell out of her bag and spilled on the edge of Aly's shoe. (Vivian was as apologetic as Grover, but Aly got the vibe that it was more about being mortified that her drink had come spilling out of her bag.) In math, she handed in her homework and talked to Kieren Jiu and his friend Douglas about some gross horror movie named *Pieces* that they'd watched on a dare. By phys ed, she was feeling good about her anger management, excited to take life as it came. She did laps around the gym with energy she didn't normally have.

Maybe I've always needed to let it flow, she

thought to herself as she jogged. *This just* feels *better. Focusing on making myself feel okay. Not worrying about whether or not I'm seen, or doing enough.*

"All right, guys, bring it in," said Mrs. Hopp, their gym teacher. She wore a purple track suit with a blue squiggle across the middle that made Aly think she looked like a Taco Bell ad from 1995 she'd seen online.

"This week, I'm going to give you a choice," she said. "Either we do volleyball in here or kickball out in the back lot. Let's vote on it. Volleyball." Hands went up. "Kickball." More hands went up. "Okay, we're doing kickball. Someone needs to go grab two balls from the equipment closet. Who's game?"

"I'll do it," said Aly, riding her wave of enthusiasm.

"You're on, Theland," said Mrs. Hopp. "Back in five."

The equipment closet was one floor down from the gym, and had the perpetual pencil-eraser smell that came with rubber balls being kept somewhere unventilated. A few other girls brushed past her, and she thought she heard her name again but kept her head up and her mind focused on getting the equipment. She even saw Rachael and two of her friends goofing off in study hall, but moved past quickly so she wouldn't embarrass her sister any further.

The push-button switch in the equipment closet lit up a single old bulb, and Aly had to peer closely to pick out the rubber kickballs from the other balls on the rack. One she found easily; the other was wedged between two pipes behind the rack, and she had to strain reaching in and pulling at it. It finally came loose all at once, sending her stumbling backward and cursing under her breath.

She stopped herself as she felt frustration rush through her. Deep breath. Felt good to finally yank the ball out. And now she was grateful she had it.

See? Little things.

The door clicked shut behind her. Aly spun, terrified that it had swung shut on its own, that she'd have to bang on the door until Mrs. Hopp came storming down.

Grace Gregor, Jess's older sister, stood with her back to the door, arms crossed in front of her.

The inside of Aly's stomach suddenly felt like it was made of cold stone. *If only the door had just swung shut*, she thought.

Even when she and Jess had been friends, Aly had always been freaked out by Grace. She'd gotten big early, tall and loping and corded with muscle from playing on the varsity soccer team. But she'd also gotten moody and would snap at Jess or call her ugly names for almost no reason. Sometimes, when Jess or Aly would make a joke and laugh, she'd stare at them in silence as though she didn't get it, or didn't want to, or was angry that they were laughing. She was a year older than Rachael but had been held back after failing three classes. There were other rumors, too, of fights, and of parents demanding she take eighth grade again so she wasn't in the same high school year as their daughters.

And here she was. Leveling those tired-looking green eyes on Aly.

Aly forced herself to keep her breathing steady. To not panic. There was a way out of this. She'd talk. She'd let it flow.

"Hi, Grace," she said.

Grace cleared her throat and said, "So, you set my sister on fire the other day. And I'd like to know why you would do that."

"I didn't do anything to Jess," said Aly. "I don't know what happened. It just—"

"Even if I believed that, and I don't," said Grace, walking slowly forward and facing off against Aly, "that wasn't my question."

Aly swallowed hard and breathed slowly.

"Jess and I were having an argument because . . . because she said some mean things about me," said Aly. "Really horrible stuff. Just because she could." Something else came to mind, and she forced herself to say it. *Let it flow.* "And I'm still angry at her for no longer being my friend. She ditched me for Athena and Kristy because I was quiet and wasn't constantly thinking about boys and which jeans would make my butt look cute. And now she thinks she's cooler than me. And it hurts. So I was angry, which is . . . why Jess might have thought I did something. But I didn't cause the fire. I don't know what did. It just happened."

Grace nodded slowly and chewed her lower lip.

"My sister has gotten *insufferable* lately, I'll give you that," she said. "Like, at what point did it become so important to be like every other girl dancing on TikTok? She sucks now. I get it."

"You do?" asked Aly.

"Absolutely. It's totally understandable."

Aly let out a shaking breath and smiled as relief washed over her. This wasn't the end of the world. Grace just wanted to set the record straight. She'd apologize for any pain Jess was going through, and—

Grace backhanded Aly so hard her teeth clicked together.

Aly wheeled and fell to the filthy floor of the closet. She rubbed her jaw where Grace's hand had hit her and tried to blink the white away from her eyes. Mostly, she felt stunned, frozen in shock. Her cheek hummed. She tasted blood in her mouth from where her braces had cut the inside of her lip.

She'd never been hit before, really hit. It was terrible.

"Thing is," Grace continued, her voice gravel-sharp, "just because I don't like Jess now doesn't mean you're allowed to burn her alive. And it sure doesn't mean your sister gets to throw shade at our mom in the halls. So, even though I agree with you, I can't just let this go. I have a reputation to keep up. But since I get it, and I never really hated you, Aly, I'm going to let you pick. Either I split your lip or I give you a black eye. Then we'll call it even. You choose."

Aly looked up at Grace towering over her. She tried to see through the pain and shock, to let it flow, only she couldn't because now the river was rushing, surging, crashing against the banks. It was full of the white light that had flashed before her eyes when Grace had hit her, and now it was overflowing and all that white-hot light was spilling out into Aly, filling her up, washing away her better judgment.

"Guess everyone in your family is a jerk," said Aly. "No wonder you got held back."

"Black eye it is," said Grace, cracking her knuckles. "Anything else you want to add before we do this?"

One thought came to mind. It sizzled red-hot from Aly's brain like a flaming billboard, like a fifty-foot-high neon sign exploding in a thousand sparks.

"Burn," said Aly.

"What?" grunted Grace.

"BURN!" screamed Aly.

Fire blasted out from the equipment racks.

Heat shot through the room in an instant wave, searing Aly's face. Hockey pads blackened and yielded their foam innards instantly. Volleyballs and basketballs began popping with sharp vents of air. Grace ducked down and screamed, covering her head and clenching her eyes shut, but Aly kept hers open and forced herself to watch as the anger moved through her and out into the room, engulfing everything around them in glorious flame.

Let it flow, she thought.

FIVE-ALARM

Whether it was the kickball next to her popping in the heat or Grace's scream that pulled Aly out of her trance, she wasn't sure—but all at once, the silence and slo-mo and hypnotic power of the raging flames were gone, and she was there, on the floor, in a burning room.

We need to get out now, or we'll die, she thought.

Grace was yanking the door with sharp, grunting pulls, but it wasn't budging. Aly leaped to her feet, put her hands over Grace's, and pulled with her—but the door still wouldn't move.

"It's stuck!" Grace cried.

Something from chemistry flickered through Aly's mind. Heat causes expansion. That was why all the doors in their house stuck during the humid summer months. They swelled.

They couldn't just yank it. They needed something to get at where it was swelling. Pull it away from the doorframe.

Her eyes scanned through the thick smoke filling the room.

There. A barrel full of field hockey sticks in one corner.

Aly ran to them, but by now, the smoke was as bad as the fire. Her eyes burned, and she couldn't breathe without tasting metal and dust, feeling airborne poison burn the back of her windpipe.

She grabbed two hockey sticks, ran back to Grace, and jammed them in the crack between the door and the wall as deeply as she could. Grace seemed to understand, and coughed, "Three . . . two . . . one . . . NOW!"

Grace pulled. Aly leaned hard on the hockey sticks.

The door flew inward with a cracking sound. Alarms were going off, and a sprinkler was starting to drench the equipment room.

By the time they got back upstairs, Mrs. Hopp and several kids were rushing toward the stairwell, their eyes following the billowing clouds of smoke. At the sight of the girls, Mrs. Hopp herded them into the gym, away from the fire. Aly put her hands on her knees and hacked, trying to cough the taste and pain out of her throat. Grace fell to her knees and threw up on the floor.

"Are you girls all right?" cried Mrs. Hopp, looking down the hall to the doorway of the equipment closet staircase. A horrific plastic smell began to fill the air.

Aly watched in horror, wondering what she'd done. Her eyes never left the blaze as the overhead sprinklers doused the whole gym in cold water, sending everyone scattering.

"What happened in there?" shouted Mrs. Hopp over the clanging bells of the alarm.

Out of the corner of her eye, Aly watched as Grace pointed directly at her.

The whole school stood out on the lawn, crowding aimlessly while their teachers tried to talk over kids shouting and the muffled fire alarm. A couple of jacket-less firefighters hung out on the two red trucks parked out front; one of them flirted with Ms. Dinesky, the social studies teacher. The initial panic of the fire alarm had died down, but there was still energy crackling in the air. Every so often, a loud burst of shouting or laughter would erupt from one of the gathered classes, and everyone would jump.

Aly watched the firefighters walk out the school, their cheeks smudged with black and gray, and wondered how she'd failed so terribly. She'd started the day so well, had felt so in control of her emotions . . . and now . . .

One of the firefighters—the chief? Aly thought his salt-and-pepper mustache looked official—stopped to talk to Principal Winters across the lawn. The principal said a few things . . .

And then his eyes fell on Aly.

The fire chief's eyes went to her, too. And then, she noticed, so did several other pairs. In fact, now that she looked around, she was standing in a clearing among the crowds; the kids around her had backed slowly away and were eyeing her in worry. Everyone knew something was up with her. Something to do with fire. Bad luck followed her wherever she went.

She hated it, but for once, Aly didn't want to feel invisible. Instead, she met the principal's eyes with a cool stare. She glowered at the kids who gawked at her, making them turn away with pink cheeks of embarrassment.

Let them look. They couldn't even understand what they were seeing. And if they had any brains about them, they'd be afraid.

As her eyes scanned the crowds, looking for any other rubberneckers to stare down, she found Simon among the kids in his grade. He looked freaked out, clutching his arms around himself and peering through the crowds. The sight of him so shaken bugged her. She headed toward him, and thankfully, anyone who saw her coming stepped out of her way.

"Simon," she said.

Simon jumped and whirled. When he saw her, his eyes went huge.

"Hey, dude," she said. "You okay?"

She took a step toward him, but he stepped back and hugged himself a little tighter.

The gesture stopped Aly in her tracks. She searched her brother's expression and saw nothing but terror. Simon was staring at her frantically, as though he wasn't sure it was her, like maybe there was some sort of monster disguised as Aly approaching him.

"Hey, it's okay, it's me," she said softly. She forced a smile. "This is unbelievable, right? I wonder when the last time was that a fire engine came to this school—"

"Did you set the gym on fire?" asked Simon.

Her mouth opened . . . and closed, and opened again. "No," she said, shaking her head. "No, it wasn't like that, it just . . . something must have . . . a gas pipe must have burst, or—"

"WAY TO GO, PYRO!"

The call cut through the air and resulted in a wave of laughter across the entire school. Aly spun, trying to see the person who had shouted it, trying to catch someone staring at her, but now they were all staring, all laughing. It was as if they were happy that someone had finally said it.

When she turned back, her brother was gone.

BURNED OUT

School was canceled for the rest of the day—the fire department said that burning gym mats might have released some toxic fumes into the building—so Mom came to pick them up. Once they were all loaded into the car, Principal Winters called out to Mom, and the two had a talk a few yards away that involved a lot of worried glances back at Aly. Rachael put an arm around her shoulder and whisper-asked if she was okay, but Aly just shook her head and kept quiet. On her other side of the back seat, Simon wouldn't even look at her.

The drive home was silent. When they pulled up to their house, a big white van with a ladder on top was parked in their driveway.

"I forgot to mention," said Mom softly, "Uncle Marco and his guys are here finishing up Aly's room."

As they piled into the front living room, four big men in paint-flecked T-shirts and jeans came trundling down the stairs, their belts and pockets clinking with screws, tools, and nails of various sizes. They waved at the kids and said something in an Eastern European language; the one with all the neck tattoos and the beard pointed at Aly and said, "All done! Looks *good*!"

Last came their Uncle Marco, like Dad but two notches looser. He had a face for smiling, with a sharp chin and a halo of curly hair. He was tough from years as a contractor but always had an air of fun about him, a gleam in his eye and curl to his smile. Dad often said he needed to take things more seriously, but Aly hoped he never did.

"Thank you, Marco," Mom said. "As always, it is amazing having a handyman in the family."

"Ain't no thing, Gretchen," he replied. "Me and the guys are playing pool at Black Rooster on Tuesdays, by the way. Tell my wacker half that if he doesn't show his face, we'll all take it really personally and softly weep about how he's forgotten us."

"I'll pass on the message," Mom said.

Marco turned to the kids and eyed them one by one.

"Simon, dude, you are *huge*," he said. "Someday, you're going to be big enough to beat me up, and on that day, I crawl beneath my porch and never emerge."

"Hi, Uncle Marco," said Simon.

"Rachael, you're looking current as always. Please give me some tips on how to take fashionable selfies for my MySpace. BFF ROFL, am I right?"

"I want to be a nun now," said Rachael. "Thanks, Uncle Marco."

"Go with God, child. And you!" Marco smiled at Aly and put a hand on her shoulder. "Kid, walk with me. We gotta talk about your room."

When they got outside, Marco said, "First of all," and began pulling up his sleeve.

"Please don't," said Aly.

"Still here!" he said, pointing at the faded black death-metal logo along his forearm.

"I get it," groaned Aly. When she was three, she'd seen Marco the day after he'd gotten the tattoo. Her uncle had been so proud of it, but Aly had loudly said, *When will you wash that ugly thing off?* Mom and Dad had applauded. Now he had to show her it hadn't washed off. Every. Time.

"Still a work of art," said Marco, slapping the tattoo.

"Yeah, okay," said Aly. "Do you even know what that says?"

"It says Cryptopsy, and don't be a wiseacre. You kids. Your generation loves to tear an old man down."

"Not as much as you love *Cryptopsy*, apparently."

Marco snickered, put an arm around her shoulders, gave her a squeeze. But when he drew back, Aly could see that something was bothering him. He stared off into space, but his eyes did little flickers back and forth, like he was seeing data in the distance.

"How'd it happen?" he asked.

"It was an accident." Aly tried to remember

Simon's ridiculous story. "There was this pair of strike-anywhere matches—"

"Aly, I'm not your parents. I've set a fire or two, okay? You didn't cause the kind of damage I saw on your wall and ceiling with matches." He squinted. "It have something to do with the bruise on your cheek?"

Aly touched the place where Grace had slapped her, tried to think of an excuse . . . and drew a blank. It was his eyes. *Somewhere in there*, she thought, *her uncle knew*. She didn't know how. She didn't know if he knew everything *exactly*. But it was as though he could see the answer in her mind and was waiting for her to let it out in the open.

"It was an accident," she repeated.

After another second, Marco sighed and slapped her on the shoulder. "Okay, welp, if anything else comes to mind, let me know, okay? In the meantime, it may smell a little burnt in there for a couple of days." He sighed. "From the matches."

She watched him walk to the van, and then rushed inside and up to her room, desperate for a moment alone to catch her breath.

THE HOT SEAT

"Have you seen my daughter's face?" yelled Mom on the other side of the door.

The waiting room outside Mr. Kunhalder's office was way worse than the principal's waiting area, Aly decided. At least with the principal, there were just piles of paper and pictures of previous graduating classes and Ms. Beal, his assistant, typing away and occasionally checking her Etsy where she sold ceramic mugs. It was all business. If you were there, well, you were probably in trouble.

But Mr. Kunhalder was trying to be sympathetic and thoughtful with his decor. Aly sat on an old over-stuffed couch instead of a wooden bench. There was a poster of two beagle puppies wrestling, with a caption that read TAKE TIME, LOVE LIFE. There was a vase full of wildflowers, all thin and violet and reedy. He even had a fish and a hermit crab in a small tank. She got the vibe that the message here was *We're just trying to figure out who you are. You're not in trouble.*

But that was a lie. She knew that being here meant she was in even worse trouble than before. She knew that this was deep trouble. Life trouble, upset-parents trouble.

At least it sounded like Mom was standing up for her in there. No matter how the fire had started, it was pretty obvious that the yellow-brown mark on Aly's cheek hadn't come from the heat in the equipment closet.

The door clicked open, and a soft voice said, "Aly? We're ready for you."

The counselor's office was narrow and painted an

overwhelming coral pink. Mr. Kunhalder sat behind a typical desk, all soul patch and green tie, with a window at his back. He smiled warmly at Aly as she took a seat next to Mom. Mom did her best to focus on the floor, but Aly could see by how she chewed her lip and wrung her hands that she was dying to ask her what had happened.

"Hi, Aly," said Mr. Kunhalder. "I don't think you've ever been here before."

"I have not, no," said Aly.

"And that's okay," said Mr. Kunhalder, spreading his hands as though to show he had nothing up his sleeve. "Not everyone has to come here or see me. But it's also really important that when someone does, they feel they *can* talk to me. I hope you feel that way."

"Sure," said Aly. The very idea made her squirm in her seat.

"Good," he said. Then he sighed and turned to the paper on his desk. "Now, look, Aly, the reason you're here is that we're worried about you. We've had three pretty major accidents lately. And they all involved two things: fire and you."

This is it, she thought. They'd finally put it together.

How could she have thought that she'd get away with it? Even if there was no provable way she could have set the fires she was being accused of . . .

A wave of contempt made Aly's brow furrow. They had nothing. What, did she spray Jess's backpack with gasoline while no one was looking? Did she booby-trap the equipment closet knowing Grace would go after her? And this wasn't the principal she was talking to—it was the school counselor. He was worried she was having psychological problems . . . and he was coercing her into saying exactly what she was about to say. Owning up to it. Playing into his hand.

"I don't know what to tell you," she said calmly. "I had nothing to do with those fires."

Mr. Kunhalder sighed. "Aly, communication and honesty are an important part of—"

"Are you calling me a liar?"

"Aly," whispered Mom, but Aly could see that she'd gotten to him—Mr. Kunhalder's mouth hung open for a second, and he blinked quickly behind his glasses. Seeing him flabbergasted made her think of Rachael and her bossy manner. How often had her sister drawn those kinds of looks from people who underestimated her?

"Not that you're *lying*, exactly," he said, "just maybe that you think the truth will cause you problems, and—"

"How am I supposed to have caused the fire in the equipment closet?" asked Aly. "I was there, and given how quickly that fire spread and how hot it got, I don't think a few matches or a Bic lighter would've caused it. And why, if I was trying to burn it down, would I do so with me inside?"

Mr. Kunhalder chewed his lip. She had him there. He had no proof. Someone had told him to get the truth out of Aly, and she wasn't biting.

"Then how do *you* explain the fires, Aly?" asked Mr. Kunhalder.

The man's tone made Aly bristle. "I don't know, Mr. Kunhalder. I'm not an expert in starting fires. Why don't you ask Grace Gregor? Maybe she learned it during her first round of eighth grade."

"And for the record," said Mom, shooting a hard glance at the counselor, "Grace isn't walking away from this without punishment."

"Definitely," said Mr. Kunhalder. "But right now . . . well, we just have a lot of questions that have no answers, Aly. And given that they all involve you—"

"They all involve a lot of things," Aly interrupted.

"We're just trying to help, Aly," said Mom. She put a hand on Aly's shoulder, but in her righteous anger, Aly shrugged it away.

"Here's what I know," she said, feeling driven by her anger in a good way, a strong way. She had to be careful, lest she start a fire in the office . . . but it didn't feel like that kind of anger. She was in control here. "Three times in the past week, I've been bullied at this school. This"—she pointed at the yellow bruise that she knew lined her cheek—"came from being slapped so hard by Grace Gregor that I nearly passed out. Each of those times, the teachers didn't seem to notice anything—and then, when fires broke out, suddenly I'm the only person they wanted to talk to? Maybe you should bring your staff in here, and ask *them* about the fires. Maybe you should bring the Gregor sisters in here and ask them. Because unfortunately, I've got nothing else for you."

"No one's saying you're the bad guy here, Aly," said Mr. Kunhalder.

"How can I be?" she said, standing. "I didn't do anything." She turned and strode out of the office, the speechless looks on the grown-ups' faces shoveling coal into the engine of her heart.

As she walked through the school, rumors and gossip swirled around Aly like background music. She could feel it everywhere, the pointed fingers and stage whispers and poor retellings of the supply closet fire. But for once, she didn't care. In fact, she kind of enjoyed it, knowing that so many people were discussing her. She felt like the problem child, the supervillain, enjoying the shocked stares of people who had no idea what was really happening.

All she could think about for the rest of the morning was telling Rachael about her meeting with Mr. Kunhalder. She could see it now—the raised eyebrows giving way to the sly smile, the too-tight hug, or the too-hard pat on the back that told her how much her sister approved. She'd done something Rachael-worthy, and wanted to share her feeling of triumph with the only person who she thought would understand it.

She knew Rachael had math before lunch, and so she went and waited by her classroom. The bell rang, and her classmates filed in—each of them looking at Aly the way one might look at an armed guard—but no Rachael. After another five minutes, she headed toward the eighth-grade lockers, wondering if maybe her big sister was scrambling to get her books. Or cutting class. The latter had happened before.

She turned a corner, saw Rachael by her locker, opened her mouth—and froze.

Rachael loomed over a boy from her grade, Kristoff Parker. Until recently, Aly would've considered the kid a fellow in invisibility, a quiet boy who mostly ran the school's AV club.

The way he stared up at Rachael worried Aly. It was the expression of someone helpless, someone who saw no way out. She knew the feeling.

"I'm sorry, Rachael," said Kristoff. "I just couldn't get it on time without Mr. Bewson noticing."

"You *said* you could get it," said Rachael. "You said it maybe six or seven times. What's the issue?"

"It's harder than I thought," squeaked Kristoff. "The camera you want is new—"

"I didn't come here for excuses," she snapped.

Aly took a step back around the corner and put her back to the wall. So it was happening again— Rachael using her popularity to boss kids around. It had become a big deal last year, when Rachael had convinced a girl in her class, Rhonda Sawyer, to do her science homework for her. Rhonda's mother had complained. Mom and Dad had been upset.

And now Kristoff. Trying to get a camera. Aly almost didn't want to know what it was for—

"You know who my sister is, right?"

Boom.

Aly's breath hitched in her chest.

It couldn't be. Rachael would never—

"Y-yes," whispered Kristoff.

"And have you heard what my sister does to people who mess with our family?"

Even from around the corner, Aly could hear the boy gulp.

"She sets them on fire," he mumbled.

"Now, I would never say such a thing out loud,"

said Rachael. "I would never tell you that messing up again might result in the AV room bursting into flames with you inside it. I'm just saying that if the next time I find you, you have the camera and the extra memory card ready, it will make me really happy. And then Aly will be happy. Got it?"

"Got it," he mumbled.

Aly couldn't take any more. She peeled herself off the wall and escaped down the hallway, her excitement and pride sinking into the whirlpool of sadness inside her.

SICK BURN

The rest of the day was a blur. Blast after blast of confusion and disgust rocked Aly. In her sadness and disappointment, she found herself regressing back into her natural middle-child state. She kept her head down and her mouth shut. The web of gossip around her was no longer empowering; now it was like the thornbush in "Sleeping Beauty," closing in and making her worried it might cut her if she moved the wrong way.

The whole car ride home, Rachael talked about

Jamal Greenblatt, a boy in her class who she'd decided was "really interesting." Mom watched Aly in the rearview but said nothing to her.

At least my visit with the counselor means I can be sullen and she doesn't ask why, Aly thought.

Once they got home, she went to her room, dropped her bag, and paced a few minutes. She took a deep breath, tried to enjoy the feeling of being home from school, thanked the universe for . . . for . . .

She couldn't think of anything. The exercise felt stupid. Rachael using her as a threat had sucked all the joy out of her life. She tried to let it flow, but it carried her straight into Rachael's room, bathed in the scent of Lavender Sunrise and Autumn Hayride.

"Hey, all good today?" asked Rachael as Aly closed the door behind her. "I heard you had to talk to Kunhalder—"

"You used me," snapped Aly, jabbing a finger at her sister. "You used me to get what you wanted. I should have known."

"Whoa, whoa, whoa, what is this?" said Rachael with a little laugh. "Als, I would never—"

"You threatened Kristoff Parker in the hall today.

You told him I'd burn him if he didn't get you some kind of camera."

Rachael's face fell into a tight, frustrated smile. Aly could read it plain as day—*Well, you caught me red-handed.*

"It's not a big deal," Rachael said softly. "I'm starting a TikTok, and I want it to be really professional, so I just need a better camera than my phone—"

"You *told him I'd hurt him with my powers*, Rachael! The whole school thinks I'm a pyromaniac freak, Mom is losing her mind worrying about me, and you're telling people I'm going to burn them alive . . . so you can get a *camera*?"

"A really *good* camera, though," said Rachael, pulling the handheld camcorder from her backpack. "This thing has ultra-HD capacity. My feed is going to look straight-up cinematic."

"Oh God." Aly felt tears bite the backs of her eyes as it dawned on her. "This was never about helping me, was it? You just wanted to make sure my powers were real so that you could use them to get what you wanted."

"First of all, that's really unfair and hurtful," said

Rachael, putting a hand to her chest. "All I've done so far is try to help you, Als. We breathed together, we researched your power—I thought we were really connecting over this."

"Then why—"

"*Second*," Rachael pushed on, "since we've established that you do have these incredible powers, why not use them? Why not get what we want? If the whole school is going to be scared of you like a bunch of witch-hunting Puritans, I say we let them know that they might get burned if they don't fall in line."

"How can you say that, Rachael? I can't control this! I nearly killed Grace Gregor! Simon's *terrified* of me! My whole life is falling apart, and all you can see is how it would benefit *you*."

"*Us*, Als? I'm thinking of you in all this. You want your favorite seat in the library? A hard stare and it's yours. You want some creep like Ray Westra to leave you alone? Boom, he's gone! Aly, you're like a *god* or something—"

"I don't buy it," said Aly. And suddenly, like her rage in the gym equipment room, words she'd swallowed for years came pouring out. "It's always for you.

Your number one priority is *always* yourself. This is all about you getting *your* way."

Rachael's mouth fell open, and she put a hand to her chest. "*Wow*. I'm pretty sure spending my afternoon in the woods helping you *literally put out fires* wasn't all about me, right? I didn't have to do all those breathing exercises and everything with you. I did them because I care about you. See what happens the next time you get so angry that you burn down a building and I'm not there to help you. We'll see how cool Simon thinks you are then, and I won't be coming to lend you a hand."

Aly felt her face scrunch up like a fist. She hated her sister, hated the way she played on Aly's insecurities and made *her* out to be the bad guy. She felt her rage build, concentrate into a single ball, and expand outward, filling her ears, making her blood pound so loud she thought she might burst . . .

And then it hit her.

"Why not now?" she asked.

"What are you babbling about?" asked Rachael.

A breath rushed out of Aly, deflating the ball of fury inside her. She sagged under her feelings.

"Why isn't anything burning now?" asked Aly. She ran a hand across her sweaty brow and into her hair. "I'm furious at you. I feel more like I could burst than ever before. But nothing's happening." She let out a dry laugh. "Maybe I'm over it. Maybe I can keep it bottled up in a way that I couldn't before—"

Fwumpf! The girls reared back. The corner of Rachael's homework blackened and curled inward as an orange flame sprouted out of it. Rachael cried out, grabbed her pillow, and began swatting at the paper with it.

"Stop it, Aly!" she cried.

Aly took a step back and held up her hands. "I'm not doing it," she said.

"Please, Aly, please!" shrieked Rachael, tears flying off her cheeks as she tried to smother the blaze. "I'm sorry, okay?"

"I'm not doing anything," said Aly. Somehow, she knew she wasn't. Her anger was all soft around the edges, nowhere near the flowing river of fury that had possessed her the previous times she'd used her power. But if not her, then how? Maybe the power wasn't even hers to control anymore. Maybe fires would just start happening in her wake, whether she liked it or not.

The idea made her clap a hand to her mouth. A human lava flow. A river of fire, burning everything in her path.

Finally, Rachael grabbed a glass of water from her desk and threw it on the flames, dousing them with a sizzle. Then she spun and faced Aly with a look of bitterness and outrage.

"I said I was sorry!" she shrieked. "Oh my God, what's wrong with you?"

"I . . . I don't know what happened," said Aly.

"Get out!" said Rachael, pointing to the door. "Leave me alone!"

Aly ran to her room, nearly mowing down a worried-looking Simon in the hall. She locked her door, flung herself onto her bed, and covered her head with her pillow, trying to smother the flames in her mind that somehow still raged.

FIRE ESCAPE

Something was off.

Aly sat up in bed on Monday morning and groggily glanced at the light spilling in between her curtains. It was too bright, she realized—too late in the day for it to be her normal six-thirty wake-up time. Something wasn't normal.

She grabbed her phone off her bedside table, pressed the home button—

8:02?

She'd slept in. She was late.

Instinct kicked in all at once. She was on her feet, riffling through her dresser, trading pajamas for the quickest, easiest outfit she could find. No time for new jeans—she grabbed the ones on the floor from yesterday, yanked them on, cursed her messed-up hair in the mirror, and—

Someone knocked at her door.

She froze, disheveled and blindsided, midway through trying to wipe down her bed head.

"Uh . . . yes?"

The door cracked a hair.

"Hey, hon, it's Mom."

"I know I'm late, just give me five more minutes—"

"You're not late." Mom cracked the door a little wider, peeked her head in, and gave Aly a tight smile. "Your father already took Rachael and Simon to school. I figured that, with everything going on right now, you could use a day off."

"Oh." Aly slowly unwound the spring inside her, felt her muscles relax, her arms drop at her sides. "That's really cool, Mom. Thank you."

"Don't get too used to it. But right now, it seemed

appropriate. Your gran would do it for me, too, when I was having a rough time." Mom's eyes went to the floor, and she took a preparatory breath. "No pressure, but I was thinking we could do something. Go to the bookstore, or just a walk or something. But the day's yours to have, so for the record, whatever you want to do is fine by me."

"No, that'd be really nice." Aly looked around her room, at her mismatched outfit and poofy-haired reflection. "Just give me a second to get dressed, okay? Sorry, I didn't expect to have the day off."

"Take all the time you need," said Mom. "It's your day."

Mom made her peanut butter toast and a banana-strawberry smoothie, and they ate on folding chairs in the backyard. The sky was overcast and gray but dry and not too cool—*the kind of day*, Aly thought, *that she needed*. No extremes in any direction, just calm and full of shade.

After breakfast, she sang *Hamilton* in a long, hot shower, then returned downstairs in a hoodie and pajama pants. Mom laughed at the fashion choice—"Man, when you take a day off, you don't pull any punches!"—and changed into her own sweatpants. Then they drove to Main Street and hit the used bookstore. Aly ended up grabbing two books, one on meditation practices, the other a novel about a family with an evil, psychic dog. She figured the first might give her good advice about how to better control her powers while the second might distract her from everything going on in her life. Mom seemed surprised by the choices but didn't say anything as the hunched old woman at the register rang them up.

For lunch, they got Aly's favorite, Tacos de Excelencia. About two-thirds of the way through their smothered burritos—carnitas for Aly, tongue for Mom despite Aly's gagging and head shaking—Mom put down her utensils, wiped her hands, and leaned in close.

"Can we talk?" she said. "Like, real talk. No dancing around the issue."

Aly's chewing slowed. She looked into her mother's eyes and saw genuine concern, not just the solution-chasing that Rachael was all about. Slowly, she nodded.

"Maybe the worst thing I can do is pretend like I

know exactly what you're going through," said Mom. She stared off into the distance and shook her head at something Aly couldn't see. "It didn't help me when I was your age. If anything, it just drove me further away from everyone I knew because it was obvious that they were just saying that without *actually* understanding my life. So I withdrew. I went underground. Didn't talk to anyone. Didn't let anyone in. Problem was, one day, when I had reached the point where I *could* deal with my own issues, everyone was scared that I didn't love them. That I didn't want them around."

The pork felt dry in Aly's mouth, and swallowing it took effort. "You're worried I feel that way about you."

"Actually, I'm not," said Mom. "No matter what's happening, that experience taught me that people don't change overnight, even if it seems like they do. I know that no matter what's going on right now, my beautiful, brilliant, shining fellow middle child is still there. And she's still absolutely wonderful."

Aly's cheeks simmered. She told herself it was just hot sauce. "I appreciate that."

"It's just the truth," said Mom. "But look, I bring

this up for three reasons. First, I want you to know I'm trying to get there, even if I fail left and right. Second, I want you to know that no matter what's going on right now, I still love you because I know you're my Aly. And third, I just want you to know—I *promise* you—that there's a light at the end of the tunnel. It took me many years and a lot of stupid wardrobe changes to figure that out, but I did." She reached out and took Aly's hands. "So just keep going. Take deep breaths, and scream if you need to, and, whatever, *meditate*." She nodded toward their bookstore bag. "But focus on the light. And know that you'll find your way out. I have no doubt about that."

Aly smiled. She almost said it then—almost clasped Mom's hands and blurted it out loud. *I'm pyrokinetic. The fires are my fault, but not like how you think.* At the last minute, though, she stopped herself. Part of it was that she knew Mom wouldn't believe her. Or if she used her powers and proved it to Mom, that would open a whole different can of worms and someone might get hurt. She knew whatever she said would end the moment she was having with her mother . . . and she would have done anything in the world to keep that from happening.

"I hear you, Mom," said Aly. She smiled big. "I'm cool."

"We don't have to keep doing that if you don't want," Mom said quickly. "I hope you never felt like I pushed the whole middle-child thing on you."

"No. You never did anything. It's just that right now . . ." Aly tried to think of how to explain her feelings to her mom without saying, *I'm doing my best not to start fires with my emotions.* "I'm trying to figure out which parts of my life I like, or need, and which parts of my life that I don't. And I like our family. I like being the middle child. I just need to understand exactly what that means, you know?"

Mom leaned across the table and gave her a peck on the forehead. "How I ended up with a daughter so levelheaded," she said, "I'll never understand."

You have no idea, thought Aly.

And . . . exhale.

The breath steadily left Aly's lungs. She felt every

inch of it, every second of air exiting her body, until she was hollow. As she exhaled, she imagined the hole in the top of her head, a great round opening like she'd seen in a picture of the Colosseum in Rome. In her mind, the anger rose in a cloud of dark smoke; her exhale cut it loose like a helium balloon, and it drifted up, up . . . and out.

Her eyes slowly opened, and she took a moment to readjust to her afternoon-lit room.

Wow! A smile crept over Aly's face as she closed her book on meditation. The techniques they'd described—focusing on the breath with her eyes closed, imagining her anger as rising heat, and picturing the pathway out of her—had all worked. She felt great, empty but in a good way. Like a huge weight had just decided to float off her shoulders.

Maybe it could work. Maybe she could keep a lid on it.

She heard the door opening downstairs just as she left her room, followed by loud, stomping footsteps. The noise was familiar—and sure enough, Rachael stormed up the stairs and beelined toward her room.

Aly took a step toward her and said, "Hey, can we talk—" but her sister only made a disgusted noise in her throat, went straight to her bedroom, and slammed the door.

Dad was helping Simon take off his coat as she came downstairs. When he saw her, he shot her something between a grin and a grimace.

"Hope your day off chilled you out because your big sis is taking no prisoners," said Dad.

"Any idea what's wrong?" asked Aly.

"Well, she was pretty dolled up and nervous when she went to school today," said Dad, "so I'm guessing a boy." He hung Simon's coat and walked off into the house, mumbling, "Poor kid."

When Aly turned to Simon, her brother was staring at her, looking a little confused. She smiled at him and said, "All good?"

"Yeah," he said with a slow nod. "You seem different. It's like something's . . . gone. It looks good."

The words made warmth bloom in Aly—not heat, not the rising flames of rage or embarrassment, but the warmth of home, of her family.

"It feels good, too," she said, trying not to get

choked up. She put a hand on Simon's shoulder. "And I'll try to keep it that way. Okay?"

"Okay," he said. "My science homework is tough tonight. Can you please help me?"

"What are big sisters for?" she said, and led him toward the dining room table.

The next morning, she almost made waffles for everyone, then stopped herself and had her own cereal instead. She helped Simon get dressed—this time, it was science class freezing him up, but her homework help made him a bit quicker to get dressed than usual. She also took extra time putting together an outfit she liked. Before leaving for school, she meditated, and once more allowed any frustrations or doubt she was feeling to drift out of her and into the open air.

It felt great, she thought. She liked helping her family, doing things for others, but she also needed to start making her own peace a priority.

The lightness carried her all the way through the ride to school, with Rachael staring sullen and silent out the window. She walked to class with her head held high, got a nod and a smile from Kieren Jiu, and even threw out a few right answers to Ms. Valez. The space where her fury had been was open now, and she was filling it with whatever she wanted.

She was on her way to the next class when the smell hit her nose. In an instant, fear and confusion flooded into her heart.

Smoke.

She told herself it was an accident. Some random burnt notebook in the chemistry labs. It wasn't her concern . . .

But she couldn't stay away.

She followed her nose. It led to the eighth-grade lockers.

Mr. Thomas, the janitor, was yanking at the door of a locker over and over with hands wrapped in big, thick gloves. Huge plumes of black smoke spilled out of the crack in the locker door and òozed from the slats. Behind him, Principal Winters stood poised with a fire extinguisher; behind them, a crowd of students watched in excitement and worry.

Finally, Mr. Thomas put his foot against the wall, pulled with all his might—

BANG, the door flew open, and out of the locker

blasted a massive fireball. Janitor, principal, and students all backed away and shielded their faces with their hands. Principal Winters swung up the fire extinguisher and blasted the locker's inside with white foam.

The scene set off a spark of panic in Aly. She shouldn't be here; sooner or later, someone was going to look away from the burning locker, see her, and think she had something to do with it. She spun around—

Kristy Schnapp blocked her path, arms crossed, nose up.

"Hope you're happy with yourself," she said.

"What—what happened?" asked Aly.

Kristy laughed. "Like you don't know. We all saw it yesterday, Aly. We saw Jamal blow off your sister. We watched her run crying from the cafeteria." She shook her head. "Me and Jess said it was only a matter of time before something of his burned. Guess his locker was your way of standing up for big sis, huh?"

Aly swerved and marched past Kristy. Her mind reeled. So many questions ran through it all at once.

Because this was different. This changed everything.

Aly hadn't burned that boy's locker. She'd had no idea that he had been mean to Rachael the day before. Heck, she hadn't even been at school, and Rachael sure hadn't told her anything about why she was upset.

But if Aly hadn't burned his locker . . . who had?

CANDLES

She didn't burst into Rachael's room or make a big dramatic show of throwing open the door. That was too much, she decided—too much drama, too much fuel for the fire. Instead, she walked in slowly and faced her sister with a head full of such post-meditation calm, not even the odor of an Alabama Honeysuckle candle could overwhelm her.

"We need to talk," Aly said.

Rachael leaped up from her bed, went to the door,

closed it, and used her key to lock them in. Then she turned and put her back against it, shooting Aly a scared look.

"You didn't have to do that to Jamal, Aly," said Rachael in a cracking voice.

"I didn't," Aly replied calmly. The feeling felt new, if not very good. For the first time in over a week, she felt entirely at ease. She'd figured out what was going on. She knew what had to be done.

"I know he was mean to me," said Rachael, looking down at the floor and nodding sadly. "Maybe that was my fault. Maybe I shouldn't have made such a big deal out of asking him out. Maybe the cafeteria was too public a place. But I didn't think you'd burn his locker!"

"I didn't," said Aly. She folded her arms.

"When I said we could do whatever we wanted, I was wrong," said Rachael. "This is wrong, Aly. You can't just—"

"Shut up, Rachael," said Aly.

Rachael gasped. "Aly, don't say that! That's mean! I'm just upset about—"

"You're not listening to me," said Aly. "I didn't burn Jamal's locker."

"Are you saying it was a coincidence?" Rachael's eyes went wide. "Do you think there's another pyro in our school?"

"No," Aly stated, studying her sister hard. She took a deep breath and finally spoke her suspicion out loud. "I think there's another one in this house. In this room."

Rachael crinkled up her nose. "I'm not following."

"Rachael, cut it out," said Aly, determined to suss out the truth. "A few nights ago, right when I was telling you I couldn't do it, your book suddenly caught fire. As if on *cue*. But none of the other times were like that. They were uncontrollable. But controlling things, making them happen the way *you* want them to . . . well, that's what you're good at."

Rachael shook her head and waved a hand at Aly. "Als, come on. Out in the woods, when I got you angry, that tree—"

"Yeah," said Aly, nodding as she remembered the way the tree had exploded into flames. How her sister had run around extinguishing them. "It did. And my desk, and your notebook the other night. All these fires have been starting *around* me. But now I'm not sure if I've been starting any of them. Because today, I tried it out, just like you kept telling me to. I went out into the woods again, and I thought about everything you said to me, and about Ray Westra, and about how *alone* I've felt this past year." Aly's eyes stung, and her voice cracked. She swallowed down the sudden rush of feelings and focused on the task at hand. "And guess what happened, Rachael. Nothing. Absolutely nothing. Not even a spark. Tell me—is it both of us? Or is it only you?"

Rachael put on a confused face and began opening and closing her mouth as if she couldn't find the right words.

Aly's stomach sank inside her.

Rachael *always* had something to say. She was *always* ready.

That was how Aly finally knew. Knew in her heart.

"It's been you," she said. "It's been you all along, Rachael. You're the one starting the fires. And you've been pinning them on me, and making me think it's been me. Even in school—you've been following me, right? You must have seen me going to the supply closet. You must have known that when I saw Ray in chemistry, he'd make some comment. And with Jess, and with Simon in the cafeteria being bullied—someone told me to come help Simon, so they must have come to you, too." Aly nodded over and over as the truth cemented in her mind. "Wow, now it really makes sense. And when I explain it to Mom and Dad, it'll make sense to them, too."

All the emotion seemed to drain from Rachael's face. She stared blankly at her sister, unblinking.

Her hand went to the light switch and clicked it off. For a moment, Aly found herself plunged into total darkness.

One of the candles on Rachael's dresser ignited with a soft pop. Then another, and another. Then the ones on her desk, her bookshelf, her windowsill, until the whole room was lit up like the inside of a church at Christmas.

Aly's eyes followed the igniting candles in a circle around the room . . . that came back to Rachael. Her sister stepped slowly and calmly into the candlelight, the dozens of tiny flames meeting in the twin blazes of her eyes.

"I'm going to be real with you, Als," she said in a soft, deadpan voice. "I think that's a very bad idea."

BURNING FOR YOU

Aly's mouth went dry. She forced herself not to back
away from her big sister, even though the emotionless-
ness of Rachael's voice and gaze downright frightened
her. She tried to think of something to say over the
pounding of her heart.

"How long have you known?" asked Aly.

"About the fire?" said Rachael. "Maybe a year.
Maybe a couple. But maybe I've always known. It

always felt like there was something better than everyone else going on inside me."

"But then . . . why?" asked Aly. "Why make me think I was the one with the power?"

Rachael nodded slowly, like she'd expected that question. "Okay, admittedly, sometimes it wasn't entirely about you. In your science class, I wanted to convince the school that there was a safety issue they needed to fix, which would cause a shutdown of all public events. And Jess Gregor was part of the May Flowers King and Queen committee, and had all the votes in her backpack. Diedre and Lauren had already heard from one of those stupid friends of hers that I hadn't won. So between those two fires, I was hoping to make people think the dance was cursed, or that it wasn't a safe idea."

For a moment, Aly thought her sister was speaking in some sort of secret code . . . and then, bit by bit, the pieces came together in her mind.

"The *April Showers Dance*?" she said with a bit of a laugh. "You set people on fire and wrecked my life because you weren't going to be voted May Flowers Queen at the dance?"

"*Initially*," snapped Rachael, pointing at Aly as though she was offended at being misconstrued.

"But you said in the car that you *didn't care* about the dance. You said there were more important things going on."

"There were," said Rachael with a glimmer of a smile. "There *is*. And it's you, Als."

"What does *that* mean?"

"Something clicked when I saw you stand up for Simon in the cafeteria," said Rachael, smiling and shaking her head. "Up until then, no offense, you'd kind of just been a means to an end. I torched your room to make you think you were doing it, plant the seed in your mind, because I knew you'd suffer in silence. That's what you usually do, Aly. Again, no offense."

Aly wanted to argue, but the words wouldn't leave her mouth. She was too shocked, both by her sister's plans and her honesty.

"When you got between Bentley Moss and Simon, I saw this desire to be seen, to stop putting up with everyone else. And I realized, I'm always working so hard to be cool, to get noticed . . . and it doesn't feel real. All I want is *more*. But your feelings, Aly . . . they were so real. They're powerful, and beautiful, and *heroic*. Just like that, I knew what I wanted. What would make me happy, what would feel *real*. And that was to give you a story. A chance to feel powerful, like you could express yourself. And if the cost was following you around and burning some things, then that's what I'd do."

Rachael took her sister's hands in hers. "And you were . . . *incredible*, Aly. You were unbelievable. When I overheard you fight back against Grace, I could have cried, it was so beautiful. I threw my fist in the air. Burning that room was poetic—and watching you save Grace was even more wonderful than I ever could have imagined. Your heart is *so big*." Rachael smiled sweetly. "You're my hero, Aly. I want to be like you when I grow up. You gave me the story, really. I just provided the special effects."

Of all the explanations Aly had imagined on her way into her sister's room, this hadn't been one of them. Part of her almost felt flattered or honored that her big sister had been so enamored of her and thought she was so genuine . . .

And then she remembered the equipment closet. The smoke stinging her lungs. The look on Grace's face as they both thought they might die.

"You could've *killed* someone," Aly said.

Rachael rolled her eyes. "Who? The guy who's been torturing our brother? Your ex-friend, or her sister who mutilated your face? These people couldn't bother to be decent, Aly—so forget them! Besides, no one was going to die. I always had it under control."

"Under control?" Aly laughed. "It didn't seem very under control to—"

Rachael snapped her fingers.

All the candles went out at once . . . except for a single flame dancing on the tip of her index finger.

She snapped again, and the candles relit. She clapped—and suddenly a candle flame danced over the end of each of her fingertips. She clawed her hands, and the fire darted between her palms and swelled into a fireball. Aly couldn't take her eyes off the rolling flame moving between Rachael's hands, an ever-crashing wave of light and heat.

"Oh God," Aly whispered.

"That was the one thing I couldn't do for you, Aly," said Rachael. "Making it look like you controlled the fire was too hard. And honestly, it didn't track with your character. I mean, you act like you can control your emotions, but I knew you were fit to burst. But don't you worry. I'll always make sure you're safe. You'll never get burned."

Rachael stepped back and drew one hand from the contained blaze. A single candle flame floated in her palm, a tiny petal of fire. She reached out and gently sent it floating across the room toward Aly. Dumbfounded, Aly held out her cupped hands to receive it, mind blank at the magic of the scene.

The flicker of flame touched down in her grip, illuminating her balled hands like a lightning bug—

"OW!" Aly yanked her hand away, her fingers burned by the airborne flame. The glimmer of fire disappeared instantly.

"Sorry," said Rachael.

The shock of the pain pulled Aly out of her numb fascination. A million emotions flooded her at once, and the smell of three dozen seasonal scented candles became suffocating instantly. She barreled to her sister's door and tried the knob twice, frantically, before Rachael calmly walked over and unlocked it for her. Then Aly flew out into the daylit world, which felt crisp and cold on her skin.

CONFLAGRATION

Her sister had superpowers.

The thought ran through Aly's head yet again as she mentally replayed the scene in Rachael's room. She walked aimlessly around their neighborhood, happy to be out of the house, but she barely noticed anything around her, the approaching gray evening or her neighbors' yards or the occasional vaulted sidewalk slab that made her trip absentmindedly.

Watching Rachael pass her that flame had been

like something out of a fairy tale. But like all fairy tales, it had been both beautiful and scary. Even if Rachael had powers, she was also a thirteen-year-old girl who'd almost hurt people over not getting to wear a crown at a school dance. She'd melted a boy's shoes from across the room. She'd made a supply closet burn white-hot from outside a closed door. Fire was so powerful and destructive, and Rachael could wield it like it was a new phone. It was a tool. A means to an end. It was nothing like Aly's release of the power, a red-faced scream of emotions that burned the air around it.

Well, not your *release,* quipped a voice in her head. *You never did anything.*

She tried not to feel so disappointed.

Scaring people and getting in trouble at school had been frustrating and upsetting . . . but something about being pyrokinetic had made her feel incredible. A standout. More than just an invisible girl. There'd been a poetry to it—of course the fires came from the quiet one, the one no one suspected, whose feelings finally came bursting out of her in waves of blistering flame.

But it had been Rachael all along. Aly had always

been just Aly Theland, everyday middle child. It was Rachael, the popular one who was secretly angry that she wasn't *more* popular, who had the power. Merciless, destructive, wanting more and more, Rachael was basically fire in the form of a teenage girl.

Nothing had changed.

Well, not nothing. Maybe something had changed in her. Just because she wasn't able to start fires with her mind didn't mean she was unable to do something about the feelings that had been building up inside her.

Feelings that Rachael had noticed. That she'd been drawn to.

It didn't track with your character.

The words left a sour taste in Aly's mouth.

Something was wrong with her older sister. Even when she'd been bossy and opinionated and mean in the past, Rachael had never been as cruel and deluded as she was now. Now things were different. She'd threatened Kristoff Parker, she'd scared so many people, and she'd completely used Aly. This wasn't Rachael's usual level of control and intensity; even when she'd bullied kids in the past, she'd done it by pressuring them or promising them an in with her and her friends.

It was up to her, Aly realized. She needed to help her sister get to the bottom of this. Whether or not Rachael could control the fire wasn't just the issue—it was whether or not Rachael could control herself.

Aly had to talk to somebody. Somebody who understood. And she had only one idea of who.

After her long walk, she sneaked back into the house and got Dad's iPad in the kitchen. Aly plugged in the ingenious pass code of 123456 and found the number she needed in his contacts.

Up in her room, door closed, blankets over her head, she made the call. The phone rang once, twice . . . and then a click, and a grunt.

"Yallo?"

"Uncle Marco?"

"What—Aly?" Marco chuckled on the other end of the phone. "Hey, kid, what's happening? Should we FaceTime so you can see my tattoo—"

"Uncle Marco, what did you think happened in my room?"

Silence.

"What are we talking about here, kid?" asked Marco.

There, in his voice. The same tone Aly had heard when she'd spoken to him at the house.

He knew. He knew *something*.

"You seemed skeptical of my story with the matches," said Aly, trying to keep the quiver of fear out of her voice. "And, just, something happened, recently, and it got me wondering . . . What were you thinking? What scared you?"

Another pause.

"The fire is a parasite."

A chill ran through Aly in a powerful wave. She felt her breath hitch. It was Marco's voice on the other end, but all the joy had left it. Instead, something cold and terribly honest lay at the core of his words.

"What?" she asked.

"It's easy to think of it as a part of you, but it's not. It feeds on you because that's what fire does. Works through fuel. Spreads as far as it can. Burns everything in its path. You might think you're in control of it, Aly, but it'll control you. One day, you'll wake up and see the ash on your hands, and not remember what happened last night. Because the fire took over. Because it was calling the shots."

She rubbed her hands together, trying to stop their shaking, to get feeling back in her fingers. "Okay, uh . . . so how—"

"It took a hypnotist, for me," said Marco. "Really nice woman. She put me under four times, and finally it took. She put a block in place. I don't know what exactly she did. The third time, I couldn't remember my dog's name for a couple of days, and I kept making fires happen. Big fires, whole buildings. It's really dangerous. But the fourth time, it worked. If you need to take action, well, that's an option. It worked for me."

"Uncle Marco, something bad is happening," whispered Aly. "Can I come see you?"

"I'm sorry, kid, but I can't help you," he said.

"Please—"

"*No.*" He practically yelled it. "No, Aly, it . . . it took me a long time to figure it out, but I did it. I'm in control now. But what I've heard and read online is that if someone like us gets near another person like us, our fire can restart. We set each other off, and it spreads. And I can't risk that. Not after everything I went through to put out my fire. Please forgive me, but no. I can't."

Aly gulped. "I'm scared someone's going to get hurt."

"You should be," said Marco, and then the phone went dead.

FIGHT FIRE WITH FIRE

**Her next morning was a blur. Rachael spent the car ride acting like nothing had happened. Whenever Aly glanced over at her, Uncle Marco's words echoed through her head and she looked quickly away.

A *parasite*.

Could she see it in her sister? Rachael looked no different, except that maybe she'd been a little calmer than normal, a little less animated. But it should have been the opposite, right? Shouldn't the fire inside have made her angrier? Hotheaded? Instead, Rachael looked like she'd achieved a new level of zen. When she hopped out of the car, she didn't even look back or say goodbye to her parents or siblings.

The school buzzed around Aly during classes—people whispering, pointing, mentioning Rachael's argument with that Jamal kid in the cafeteria—but Aly didn't care. There was so much more at stake. She'd never heard her uncle sound scared at all, much less as terrified as he'd sounded on the phone with her. This was bad. She didn't know what to do.

She was so numb that she didn't even notice where she was walking until she turned a corner and found the eighth-grade lockers in front of her. The one that had burned the day before was blackened, with two yellow strips of caution tape forming an X over the front.

The sight of it stopped Aly in her tracks. She remembered her sister's routine the day before, the way Rachael had played the part of frightened bystander right up until Aly had called her out. She couldn't forget that Rachael had lied to her. That she'd used Aly so she wouldn't get blamed for her own selfish actions—

"Returning to the scene of the crime, huh, pyro?"

Aly's eyes darted across the hall. Three eighth-grade boys stared at her, two of them snickering and pointing. She felt her cheeks go red and pulled her backpack tight against her back.

"Oooh, now she's shy," said another one. "But when she's sticking up for her sister, that's when the gasoline comes out—"

"Cut it out," said the third boy. He stepped around his friends and approached Aly with a wave. "Hi, Aly. Do you remember me? Jamal?"

Aly stared at the boy's face for a second, her mind blank—and then a memory darted in. Day camp, one summer when she was maybe five or six. A bigger kid had taken the American Girl doll she'd been playing with, and this boy, a smaller version of the boy in front of her, had taken it back and given it to her.

The two shared a smile . . . and then couldn't help but look across the hallway, at the blackened rectangle amid the lockers.

"I didn't do that," blurted Aly.

"I know you didn't," he said. "Your sister did."

Jamal's words made Aly's shoulders hike and her muscles tense. She wondered if he knew, if he'd somehow seen Rachael at work. Given what Aly had seen last night in her sister's room, it wouldn't surprise her if Rachael had gotten sloppy . . .

"I mean, it's obvious, right?" he said. "She comes up to me, sits in my lap in the cafeteria, asks me out. I push her off, she flips out . . . I mean, this just felt so obvious." He gestured to the locker. "And for the record, I feel bad. I should've been nicer to her. I know she was just trying to impress me, and I don't like being mean to anyone. But the way she just kind of sat on me and started touching me—it felt weird. Everything about it felt weird."

Aly forced herself to nod. She'd sure missed one awkward display on her day off from school.

"Well, look," she said, "there are rumors going around about me—"

"Yeah, I heard those. But, Aly, you've never given me the *vengeful* vibe. Those stories sound like a bunch of accidents where you were at the wrong place at the wrong time." He shrugged and laughed. "Or you're some wild pyromaniac! I don't know. Point is, I don't think you burned my locker. This has Rachael written all over it."

She sighed in relief. Finally, someone didn't think she was the cause of all this.

"Thank you for understanding," she said softly.

"No problem," said Jamal with a smile. "Just watch out. Your sister is one intense girl. I can't imagine being her sibling."

"You don't even know," said Aly.

At lunch, Aly snuck out the back doors of the cafeteria and walked past the football field. There was a path back there through the woods, where teachers sometimes took lower schoolers to study leaves and bugs. Aly felt like taking a walk, getting some air.

As the cool woods closed in on either side, Aly felt at ease. Talking with Jamal had really opened up her mind to the possibilities of what could happen moving forward. Sure, everyone at school thought she was some kind of out-of-control firestarter . . . but who cared? All it would take was a new story and Aly would be old news.

Besides, Jamal was an example of how some people, the people who knew her and Rachael even slightly, would know that she wasn't capable of doing such terrible things. Even if she'd believed, for a second, that she was.

And Rachael . . . well, maybe things would work out. The more people knew it was her, not Aly, who was the problem, the more she might realize that using her powers to manipulate people wasn't okay.

The path opened up into a clearing with benches along the tree line. Aly remembered the area from one or two classes when she was a kid, where their science teacher, Mr. Rollins, had brought a huge bullfrog to school and fed it a worm.

She went to sit down—then leaped up with a yelp and whirled around.

The bolts in the seats of the benches were red-hot. The wood around them was blackened, making crackling noises as the heat bloomed against them.

"You *snitch*."

She knew Rachael would be behind her, but Aly wasn't expecting the look on her sister's face. The girl's eyes were wide and sad, tears sending dark streaks of eyeliner down her cheeks. Her mouth was half open, lower lip quivering. Her hair blew wildly as if tousled by a hot breeze.

"Calm down, Rachael," said Aly, feeling the temperature around her rise steadily.

"You *told him*. You ratted me out to a boy! A boy I *liked*, and who embarrassed me in front of everyone!"

"I didn't tell him anything," said Aly, putting up her hands defensively. "He guessed some things, but I definitely didn't tell him about your powers. Please, Rachael, calm down. You don't want to lose control—"

"I'm in control!" shouted Rachael, even as a row of dandelions behind her burst into flame. "I'm just angry, and betrayed, and *hurt*! You're my sister, Aly! You're not supposed to be palling it up with boys who humiliated me in public!"

"It was nothing!" cried Aly. "We just talked! Please, Rachael, deep breaths. Gratitude. Let it flow—"

"Oh, *shut up*, Als!" shrieked Rachael with an eye roll. "That was just what I told you to do to make you think you had the power. None of it works." She sneered. "I gave you *everything*. You were nobody at school, some quiet little mouse of a girl, and I gave you a story, and a life, and this is how you repay me!"

The weight of the past week seemed to crash down on Aly with Rachael's words. All at once, she couldn't take it anymore and let it rush out of her:

"All you gave me were headaches and bad dreams, Rachael!" Aly screamed back. "You used me! You used me because you wanted to do whatever you felt like and not get caught." And then, without planning, she dug deeper. "You've wasted so much of your time trying to be popular, you never grew a personality. So you latched on to mine because at least I knew who I was. Maybe I had no friends, and no life of my own, but at least I wasn't some try-hard."

It was as though every word from Aly's mouth drew a little bit more of the emotion out of Rachael's face. At the end, there was nothing, a look of blank frustration without a feeling in sight. A final tear rolled out her eye, but it hissed and turned into a wisp of steam.

Uncle Marco's words echoed in Aly's mind: *The fire is a parasite. You might think you're in control, but it'll control you.* That's what she was seeing on her sister's face now. Rachael was gone—too tired, too hurt.

It wasn't Rachael anymore.

The fire stared back at her.

"Last time I try to help someone." Rachael scowled and gestured at Aly with a clawed hand. From the burning dandelions behind her rose a flame that spun through the air in a growing spiral, building into a great jet of fire that billowed toward Aly.

Aly felt her eyebrows singe and her braces sting in her mouth as the blast of fire surged toward her.

This is gonna hurt a lot, she thought, closing her eyes.

"GYAH!"

Aly's eyes snapped back open. The fire was gone. Rachael was down on one knee, clutching her left eye. Her mouth was open, showing teeth gritted in pain. She threw her hand out again—but once more, she yelped and collapsed to the ground before the flames could even make it halfway to Aly.

Fingers gripped Aly's elbow and pulled her back into the woods.

She turned and saw Simon pulling her.

They sprinted between the trees, leaping over rocks and roots, weaving as they went. Finally, they found an overhang, a place where a rock jutted out of the earth, and ducked out of sight.

"You're bleeding," Aly panted after a moment.

"I know," said Simon, crimson dripping out his nose and down his chin. "That happens someti—"

Then his eyes rolled back into his head, and he collapsed against Aly.

BURNING DOWN THE HOUSE

The only thing she wanted to do was get Simon back to school, call the nurse . . .

But Aly stayed quiet.

Simon's eyes fluttered open. They met hers. Before Aly could put a finger to her lips, he nodded and drew his mouth tight. She pressed a tissue from her pocket to his nose and did her best to breathe quietly.

They weren't safe yet.

Sure enough, a few minutes later, she heard Rachael stomp past them on the path. She even caught a glimpse of her sister as she stalked back toward school, glancing into the underbrush as she went.

"Well, don't worry," Rachael finally called out to the trees. "It's not like I won't find you. I know where you live." She laughed at her own joke and then marched off toward school.

They waited a few minutes until Simon softly croaked, "Is she gone?"

"Yeah," said Aly, nodding. Then tears suddenly welled in her eyes, and she hacked something between a sob and a laugh. "Are you okay? Oh, Simon, I thought you might have died for a second there."

"I'm fine," he said, sitting up from her arms and rubbing his head. "Doing it too hard makes my nose bleed, and sometimes, I pass out. But I'm always fine when I wake up."

"Doing what?" asked Aly, wiping the tears from her eyes.

"What I did to Rachael." Simon chewed his lip a little, and then said, "It's like I can feel other people's minds. I can feel the different parts of them and under-stand what they're thinking or doing. Sometimes, I can even push them a little. Rachael has the fire . . . and I have this."

"So you . . . pushed Rachael?"

Simon nodded. "Just the part that makes the fire. And not very much. I'm scared I could hurt her really bad if I push too hard."

"Have you always known it was her setting the fires?" Aly couldn't really wrap her mind around what he was saying, but there was so much she wanted to know.

He shook his head and moved his arms around his knees. "I did think it was you for a bit. But then I started to notice that Rachael was around whenever I could feel whatever starts the fires. And with you, I can't feel anything." He smiled a little and wiped at his nose with his sleeve. "That's your thing, I guess. I can feel everyone else's mind, but yours is like a wall. I can't feel it or hear it or anything."

Aly slumped back against the jutting rock and tried to understand. One of them being a firestarter was hard enough to believe—a destructive freak of nature, some kind of genetic mix-up that gave her or Rachael superpowers. But now it was more complicated. Simon's ability wasn't as obvious, but from what she'd seen back there, it was still pretty powerful. And her abilities . . . well, it didn't feel like much, having an impenetrable brain. It wasn't fire casting or mind reading. But it was definitely helpful around other people like Simon.

So if all three of them had mind powers . . .

"Do our parents have anything like this?" she asked.

"Oh, Dad definitely does," said Simon, staring grimly off into space. "Dad can move things. But he doesn't know."

"About us? You and Rachael?"

"About himself."

"How is that possible?"

"He only uses it in little ways," Simon explained. "I didn't notice until my powers started working a few months ago, and I could feel it inside him. Then I saw it everywhere. He turns out lights without touching the switch. He closes doors behind him. A couple of days ago, I watched him steer the car while checking his phone with both hands. Nobody notices, because he's not lifting buildings or setting stuff on fire. It's all small."

"That can't be true," mumbled Aly . . . but she quickly realized she had no idea. She desperately tried to remember seeing her dad mess with the thermostat dial or turn up the stove with his hands . . . but she came up with nothing. Simon was right—she hadn't even been looking for it.

Dad's side. It made sense, with Uncle Marco.

At the end of the day, though, it didn't matter. Right now, they had bigger issues to deal with.

"What do we do about Rachael?" she asked.

"I don't know," said Simon softly. He hunched even farther, gripped his knees tighter. "The fire part . . . the thing in her mind . . . it's bigger now. It's bigger than some of the normal parts of her brain. It's scary."

"Uncle Marco said something about that," she said, then told her brother the story of the harrowing phone call. Simon nodded along, his eyes still staring off into some grim distance.

"Maybe we need to find her a hypnotist," Aly concluded. Then, hoping against hope, "Or maybe you could turn it off somehow. Find a way to get rid of it, using your powers."

But Simon shook his head hard. "It's too deep," he said. "It's a part of her that's attached to other parts of her mind. If I push it too far, I could hurt her really badly." He began trembling, and tears rushed down his cheeks. "I don't wanna hurt Rachael, Aly. She scares me, but she's our *sister*—"

Aly wrapped her arms around him and let him heave and sob. She absorbed his worry and sadness like she always had, only now she felt like it was more honest. With these secrets Simon had been keeping finally out on the table, it was almost like she was really hugging her brother for the first time in ages.

"No one's going to ask you to hurt Rachael," she assured him. "But I don't think we can trust her. And we need to stop her from causing fires until we're sure she's herself again. In the meantime, we need to steer clear of her."

Simon nodded, but a sad look crossed his face.

"What?" asked Aly.

"*Steer clear of her*," he said with a mirthless laugh. "She's our sister, Aly. We all have the same ride home."

*   *   *

The car ride. For Aly, it was a looming, dreadful thing, the tensest moment of a long, tense week. As she helped Simon back to school and into the nurse's office, all she could think of was the ride home with Mom. As she sat zombielike through the rest of her classes, all she could do was play out the scenarios in her head. How far was Rachael willing to go? How lost was she to the fire?

Finally, the moment came. Simon stood on the front steps of school, waiting for her but staring balefully at the car parked at the curb. Out in front stood Mom . . . and Rachael. Mom smiled and waved and looked perfectly normal, if maybe a little curious as to why her two younger children approached her looking as though they were entering a haunted house. But Rachael stared at them with a sharp, knowing smile and opened the back door of the car like a gloating warden leading the convicted into a prison cell.

She knows we're scared, thought Aly. *And she loves it.*

They rode in silence for a ways. Occasionally, Aly would glance at her brother and sister. Simon sat in the middle like a statue, practically unblinking as he forced his gaze directly at the radio. Rachael, meanwhile, stared out the window and occasionally sighed as though content.

"By the way, guys," said Mom, glancing at them in the rearview mirror, "just a reminder that tomorrow night, your father and I are going out to dinner at Le Ver. So you'll be on your lonesome."

"Right, your anniversary," said Rachael. "That's so nice. Happy anniversary, Mom."

"Thank you, sweetheart!" said Mom, beaming in the rearview. "We won't be late, so you guys just party without us. Rachael, you're in charge."

"That'll be fun," said Rachael, laying the enjoyment on thick. "I'm sure there'll be lots of cool stuff we can do together. Right, guys?"

Something about her tone stirred up sparks in Aly. Maybe whatever part of Rachael held her powers was changing her, but that tone, that oily, smirking, you-don't-even-know way she spoke, had been going on for as long as Aly could remember. Before, she'd shrugged it off as oldest-child attitude or swallowed down her dislike for it. Now the thought of letting Rachael act like she was Queen Everything, just because she could threaten them with being burned alive, made Aly sick.

She wouldn't let Rachael win. She'd think of something. Maybe Aly didn't have powers, but if the past couple of weeks had taught her anything, it was that she had a little fire in her, too.

"Can't wait," said Aly. She turned and locked eyes with her older sister. A little smile wound its way onto her face. "I have a few ideas of my own." Then she turned and stared out her own window, letting Rachael know how bored she was with this whole routine.

"Well, good," mumbled Mom after a moment. "Everyone's excited."

BACKDRAFT

Aly thought her heart might explode when the moment arrived the next night. Outside her room, the house smelled of shampoo steam and cologne—the aroma of parents on their way out. Somewhere, Dad was humming.

She passed Simon in the foyer and gave him a small nod to let him know the plan was underway.

Mom and Dad appeared in the upstairs hallway, dressed in their nice dinner clothes; Mom even wore her chunky gold jewelry, which Aly knew meant she and Dad might go dancing later. Aly and Simon told them they looked nice, then watched from the hall balcony as Rachael met them at the door.

"Remember, Simon needs to finish his science homework before he gets any screen time," said Mom.

"Mom, I've got it." Rachael laughed. "You kids go have fun. Promise I won't burn the house down."

Mom and Dad hugged her, then turned to the door. They were so busy making eyes at each other that they didn't notice what Aly saw—the door opening for them and closing behind them without Dad so much as touching it. Simon reached over and grabbed her hand, and Aly squeezed his. *I saw it*.

The minute they were gone, Simon and Aly went to Rachael's room and waited in the scented silence. Aly pulled out the yellow bottle she'd found in the garage by the grill and pushed up the plastic tip.

Her heart beat faster and faster with each footfall heading up the stairs . . . down the hallway . . . right outside the door . . .

The door opened. Aly spun. Rachael stopped and glared at them in surprise.

Aly raised the bottle and squeezed.

An arch of clear, harsh-smelling fluid went from the bottle's tip to Rachael's shirt and hoodie, all over her jeans, everywhere. Her sister tried to move out of the stream, but Aly followed her, spraying her up and down, until the bottle made a fart noise as it emptied.

Perfect, thought Aly.

"Wow, you've *ruined* this outfit," seethed Rachael. Then she sniffed the air. She pulled her shirt to her nose, took a big whiff. And she turned to Aly with a wide-eyed look of outrage.

"Lighter fluid," Aly explained. "You're drenched in it. So's the floor around you. If you ignite anything in here, there's a chance you'll catch, too. Maybe you can control fire, but that's probably a little harder when you're burning alive."

Rachael's face bunched and twisted, as though it wasn't sure how to express the sheer amount of anger she was feeling. She held out her hands in front of her in the shape of claws, threatening to grab Aly's face. Aly took a step back but kept her expression cool and firm. She wouldn't back down. Not this time.

"You think *this* is how you get me?" snarled

Rachael. Hot wind whipped through the room, blowing against Aly's hair. "I take a shower, I change my clothes, and then I'm fine. And then I come back here and torch *this whole place* with *both of you inside—*"

"Do you even hear yourself, Rachael?" This was the part Aly had been ready for. It was what she'd been training for her whole life—to be the one with the big heart, the one who took care of business with her feelings to guide her. She could keep coming at Rachael with strategy . . . or she could just talk to her human to human. "You're threatening to *kill us*. And then what— you walk out of here the only survivor? Mom and Dad are heartbroken but think it's an accident . . . and then you start another fire. Then what? Kill them, too? Cover your tracks? Burn all the people who love you, leave a trail of bodies in your wake so you can just keep burning more stuff, more lives?"

Rachael's lips drew tight, then pulled hard at the corners. She shook from head to toe, her poised posture looking suddenly rickety.

"I don't want to kill anyone," spat Rachael, and then all at once she started sobbing, her eyes and nose gushing in unison. "I don't want to hurt anyone else.

I just want to stop. But it's like I can't! Like I'm in too deep, and now I just want to destroy *everything*, and I don't know how to keep myself from being *bad*."

Rachael fell to her knees. Every bone in Aly's body told her to fall down next to her and take her big sister in her arms, just like she'd done with Simon the previous day . . . but when she glanced at Simon, he shook his head. If what he'd told Aly was true, he could feel when the fiery part of Rachael's brain was active, and no matter how sad she seemed, it appeared to be active now.

"Look, Rachael, you're not entirely to blame here," said Aly slowly and calmly. "I talked to Uncle Marco recently, and he told me that he thinks the fire or whatever it is about you that's giving you these powers, it's not normal. It takes over your mind after a while. From what he told me, he had it, too. But he stopped it."

Rachael sniffled and nodded fast and hard. "It feels that way, sometimes. Like, it hits me in a flash, and then all of a sudden fires are going that I don't remember starting."

"Well, if he could figure it out, I bet you can, too. But the first thing you've got to do is stop, okay? Stop using your powers to get back at people, or get what you want. Only use them constructively, or maybe even not at all. Marco needed a hypnotist, but I bet you can get a handle on it on your own. You're tough. You're ambitious and determined."

Rachael ran her hands through her hair and exhaled hard. "I don't know, Als. I don't know if I can stop. It feels so much like a part of me now."

"You *have* to, Rachael. For us, for Mom and Dad, for yourself!" Aly got down on one knee and locked eyes with her sister. "Is this who you want to be? Some force of destruction who wipes out anything and anyone that stands in her way? Sounds like a real lonely life."

Slowly, Rachael nodded again. She rose to her feet, and Aly rose with her.

"You're right," said Rachael. "I just . . . can we just talk tonight? Just the three of us? There's a lot I want to go over, about how the powers make me feel."

"I'd like that," said Aly.

"Okay," whispered Rachael. She used her wrists to wipe at her face. "God, I'm a mess. Can I go pee and clean up, and then we can order pizza and talk?"

"Sounds great," said Aly.

Rachael shot her a sad smile. "Thanks, Als," she whispered, and walked from the room.

"Wait!" said Simon.

"What?" Aly saw the look of stark, unblinking panic on Simon's face—

Just as she heard the door slam and the lock click into place.

HEAT RISES

"Rachael?" asked Aly. She ran to the door, twisted the knob, pulled as hard as she could—but not a chance. "Rachael, I think you locked us in. Can you open the door?

"Mmmno," said Rachael on the other side.

"Rachael, we want to help you!" cried Aly, pounding her first on the door.

"Yeah, I *get it*," groaned Rachael. "You're so ready to believe I'm this helpless victim of the fire. But guess what, Als—not everyone needs to be saved. I like the fire. I'm totally in control of it."

"What about being scared?" pleaded Aly. "Wanting a way out?"

"You're right, I said that, and apparently, that was the way to go because you bought it." Rachael switched to a whiny, high-pitched imitation: "*Now I just want to destroy everything! I don't know how to keep myself from being bad!* Really, guys? It's like you're my siblings and you don't even know me. But hey, whatever gets me away from this little intervention of yours."

"You need to stop!" Aly screamed. "You're going to hurt someone! You might *kill* people!"

"Oh my *God*, you're making this *so melodramatic*," Rachael replied. "All I ever wanted was to make you interesting. But you just couldn't handle it, and you snitched me out to a boy, and now you're trapped in my bedroom trying to give me help I don't need. I should've just stuck with my original plan, but I saw something cool about bringing you in. You know what, maybe that was my only problem.

Second-guessing my original idea. Get ready, because you're about to get really famous—"

Rachael's comment cut off in a shriek, and Aly heard her sister tumble. Glancing over her shoulder, she saw Simon hunched forward, veins bulging out his forehead. Blood ran from his left nostril, but his eyes never left the door.

"Get out . . . of my head," grunted Rachael.

The doorknob turned red-hot in Aly's hand.

Aly leaped back, crying out in pain. Already, a perfect circle of red had formed on her hand, looking raised and angry. The reaction broke Simon's concentration; seconds after jumping up to see if Aly was okay, he stumbled backward and braced himself against the bed to keep from collapsing.

"When I come back," said Rachael between heavy breaths, "we can talk about which one of you keeps doing that." Her footsteps rang fast down the hall, the stairs, and out the front door.

Aly went to Simon and helped him sit back up on the bed. She got him a tissue and wiped at his nostril.

"Are you going to be okay?" Aly asked.

"Yeah," said Simon with a nod. "That one wasn't so bad. Just need a second." He sniffed loudly and thumbed the tissue into his nose, to plug it. "I saw something in there, too."

"In Rachael's mind?"

Simon nodded even harder. "I think it was the school. The auditorium."

Aly nodded. That, plus Rachael's talk about her *original plan*, suggested what Aly had feared for a while now.

"Is the April Showers dance tonight?" she asked.

Simon shook his head. "I think it's tomorrow." Slowly, a smile crept across his face.

"What?"

"Just . . . neither of us knows when the dance is," he said. "Man, we're so uncool."

Rachael's tablet was still in her bag, so they checked the school's calendar. Tomorrow.

"Great," said Aly. "At least she's not attacking people. Honestly, as long as it's just property damage—"

"I bet there might be a guard still there, though,"

Simon pointed out. "Maybe a teacher working late, too."

The thought chilled Aly. Night watchmen, fire-fighters who got caught in the blaze, neighboring houses in the path of the spark-filled wind . . . if Rachael burned down the school, people were going to get hurt, if not killed. People might lose their homes.

All because her older sister was bitter from not being the May Flowers Queen.

They had to stop her.

How, they realized, was going to be a problem. Try as they might, they couldn't open the door. Meanwhile, the windows in Rachael's room were small and let out on a fifteen-foot drop down the side of the house. And when it came to breaking or opening anything, Aly's hand made her useless—already, her palm was blister-ing. Rachael had burned her worse than she'd thought.

They toyed with the idea of calling the cops, or at least Mom and Dad, but Simon shook his head hard.

"They won't believe us," he said. "And I don't want anyone finding out about me."

He touched a hand to his head, and his eyes glazed

over, witnessing a scene Aly never wanted to consider. She put a hand on his shoulder and nodded. "Okay, dude. But we have to think of something." She knelt down and looked in his eyes. "Have you ever been able to move things? Like Dad?"

Simon shook his head. "It's not like that. The best I can do is put an idea in someone's head. Sometimes, that works."

Aly froze. Maybe Simon had been using his powers now, because dang if she didn't have a new idea herself. "How *hard* can you put it in someone's head?"

A SNOWBALL'S CHANCE

They heard the car clearer than she thought they would. Waiting for it to arrive had been murder, twenty long minutes of sitting together in silence, wondering if they were too late, if Rachael was already standing in front of an inferno that was once their school. The silence was for the better, thought Aly. It gave Simon a moment to rest before what they were going to attempt.

The sounds continued: The car door. Footsteps on gravel. A fist pounding at their front door.

"Lil Joey's Pizza!" yelled the voice. "Got a large pie for one . . . Simon Theland?"

"Ready?" Aly asked. Simon nodded but didn't look very sure. "If it hurts too much, just stop, okay? We'll find another way."

"Right," sighed Simon. He closed his eyes hard, and his face tensed in concentration.

"Hello?" called the pizza delivery guy. He rang the doorbell a few times. "Anyone home? I've got—"

The man's shouts cut out with a squawking noise deep in his throat. Aly heard the sound of jerky footsteps. Simon spasmed, his neck a mass of cords, his eyes clenched like fists.

It could actually work.

"Okay," she whispered to Simon, "now the spare key, under the fake rock." She heard more footsteps and a faint scraping from outside. "Now the front door." Simon flexed; the vein in his forehead bulged. Metal scraped against the front door—then there was a click, and below them the door creaked open. "Good, Simon. You're doing so good. Now the stairs, one at a time." Loud, heavy footsteps moved up the stairs toward them. Blood began to drip out of Simon's nose. "Almost there . . . great. Down the hall, and to the door." The footsteps tromped down the hallway, closer, closer, until they were outside the door to Rachael's room. This close, Aly could also hear a faint choking noise coming from the man outside.

The doorknob shook. Fingers scraped at the lock from the other side.

It hit Aly so hard that she almost cried.

Rachael had taken the key. Of course she had. She was smart and had been locking her door behind her for over a year.

Aly tried to think fast. "Okay, there's no key. Maybe there's an extra one in the basement, where Dad keeps that big ring hanging from—"

BAM! The door shook. Aly jumped. *BAM!* Again. She looked at Simon and saw that her brother's whole face and neck were a red, bulging mass. Blood gushed out of his nostrils, splattering onto the legs of his pants. His eyelids were no longer closed but half open, and his eyes had rolled so far back that she could only see white lined with red veins.

"Simon, stop," she said.

Simon's body jerked; foamy spit formed at the corners of his mouth.

"Stop!" cried Aly. "You're going to hurt yourself! Please, just—"

BAM! The door blasted inward, hitting the wall with a bang. Into the room flew the pizza delivery boy, husky and scruffy in his bright red uniform jacket and cap. As he convulsed on the floor, Aly noticed that his eyes were like Simon's, fluttering and fish-belly white.

Simon flopped back onto the bed with a groan. As he did, the pizza guy blinked and sucked in a deep, sudden breath of air. He looked back and forth, mouth moving in terror but never uttering a word.

Aly leaped to Simon's side and checked on her brother. He was paler than she'd ever seen him, making the stripe of red from his nose down stand out like a flashing alarm. His small chest rose and fell quickly, and his eyes swam back and forth beneath their lids.

And then, all at once, he went still.

He's dead, she thought. *Oh, God, we killed him.*

"Simon?" she said, her voice cracking, her heart pounding—

Simon's eyes snapped open. He took a long, deep breath.

"Did it work?" he whispered.

Aly finally let out a sob and grabbed Simon tight in her arms. Her brother grunted and then weakly squeezed her back.

"I thought you were going to die."

"I'm okay," he said. "My brain's really weird, I guess." He pulled back from Aly and dragged a wrist across his mouth, smearing the blood. "We gotta go. How're we going to get to school?"

"Our bikes," said Aly, but immediately realized how weak it sounded. That would take forever. If they weren't already too late to stop Rachael, that would make them too late. But what else could they do, without getting Mom and Dad involved?

"Where am I?"

She'd forgotten about the pizza guy. She and Simon turned and looked down at the teenage boy as he blinked hard and tried to sit up on his elbows. As his eyes scanned the room and widened with horror, an idea came to Aly. It was ridiculous, outrageous, probably illegal, and kind of mean.

But it would definitely work.

"Dude!" she yelled.

The pizza guy yelped and cowered as he looked up at the two of them.

"Dude, what are you doing in our house?" yelled Aly, doing her best to look angry.

"I . . . I don't know!" the pizza guy insisted. "I think I was making a delivery, and . . . something happened! My head hurts! I don't know how I got here!"

Aly shook her head and *tsk-tsked* him. "Did you break in, dude? Into our house? This is a bad look."

"I *have no idea*!" sobbed the pizza guy. "Have I . . . was I sleepwalking? Look, guys, my name is Lewis Martinson, I'm from Glenbrook, and I'm just trying to do my job—"

"Well, look, Lewis Martinson, we'd love to forget about how you broke into our house and totally wrecked this bedroom door," said Aly, crossing her arms. "You just have to drive us to our school."

"School?" asked Lewis. "No, no way, man, I have to go to the hospital or something—"

Aly pressed on. "I bet if you drove us to school, we'd totally forget that we ever saw you. We'd write a

Yelp review about how polite and courteous you were, and how delicious the pizza was, and everything."

Lewis blinked a few more times, then began nodding hard and fast. "Fine, yeah, whatever. Just give me a second."

They pulled him to his feet, and then Aly threw one of Simon's arms around her shoulders and walked him downstairs. As they walked out the front door, she noticed their pizza lying half out of its dropped box, cheese oozing onto the front lawn.

"I should clean that up," said Lewis.

"Least of your worries, dude," said Aly. "Let's go."

FLASH POINT

"Here," said Simon, pointing. "Stop here."

Lewis pulled the car to a screeching halt a ways from the front of school. Aly was about to ask what he was doing when she saw the hole in the fence. It was ragged and random, the metal fingers of chain link all blackened at the edges, forming a perfect shape to walk through with a duck of the head. One or two of the link tips still glowed faintly orange.

"What kind of *Stranger Things* shenanigans are you kids up to?" asked Lewis.

"You don't want to know," Aly replied. She opened the door, helped Simon out of the car, and closed the door behind her. Then she went to the passenger seat window and said, "Listen, you can't tell—" But before she could finish, the car peeled away from them and sped off, Lewis shouting a rude remark at them as he left.

They walked across the back lawn by the football field. The school loomed up ahead of them, dark and still; Aly had never seen it without any people inside, and the stillness of it all chilled her nerves. It was as though the world had ended, and they were wandering through the apocalypse to a building they'd known back when everything was normal.

When they got to the cafeteria door, they found the lock and knobs melted away. Aly pushed the door open a crack, and they slipped inside and made their way to the auditorium.

The space was actually beautiful, fully lit and decorated ahead of the dance. Pink and pastel-blue streamers hung from the ceiling while giant paper flowers of various colors sat piled on the tables that lined the edges. Boxes and piles of unused materials were stacked throughout, not yet stored away before the dance the next night. The walls and ceiling were alive with string lights, which made the room glow warmly and sent flickering sparkles of light off the disco ball hanging above the stage. A giant banner overhead read APRIL SHOWERS—PUT A SPRING IN YOUR STEP.

As she scanned the room, Aly wondered where Rachael had gotten to. She'd certainly turned on the lights . . . but she was nowhere to be found.

"Simon, can you . . . feel Rachael?" she whispered.

Simon swallowed hard. "I might need a moment before I can. I don't feel so good."

"That's okay," said Aly. She patted her brother on the back and kept looking around the room, mumbling, "Rachael, where are you? Where could you possibly be?"

"I'm over here."

Aly gasped and spun. Rachael sat at one of the tables away from the stage, sipping a soda and wearing an oversized sports jersey and a pair of sweatpants.

"What are you doing?" asked Aly.

"I got tired, so I'm caffeinating," said Rachael, gesturing to her drink. "You just didn't see me because you came in here expecting some big, villainous scene." She looked down at her outfit and smiled. "Plus, I had to change to get all the lighter fluid off me. So I'm looking, like, *shabbier* than normal."

Aly sighed, and her shoulders drooped. Now that her sister had said it, that's exactly what she'd come here expecting. Rachael with a gas canister, covering the auditorium in kerosene, cackling to herself.

Instead, here was her sister. Just sitting there. Having a soda.

She and Simon walked over and stared at her for a minute. Then Simon pulled out a chair and sat down; Aly, after a few seconds, did the same.

"I take it from this"—Rachael gestured to Simon, then to her nose, motioning down her chin in the direction of their brother's blood smear—"that you're the one who brain-slapped me earlier?"

"Yup," said Simon.

"That hurt," said Rachael.

"You locked us in your room," said Simon.

"Fair," she said. "Are you okay?"

"Yup," said Simon, lowering his head to his folded arms on the table. "Just going to rest my eyes for a second. Don't burn the place down if I'm asleep."

"Deal," said Rachael. She looked over at Aly. "Still no powers for you, though, Als? Bummer."

"Rachael, listen to me," said Aly. "According to Uncle Marco, the fire isn't just a power, it's a parasite. It's taking you over and making you do things you wouldn't normally do. If we can find a way—"

"Aly, stop." Rachael stood up, walked around the table, and sat down next to Aly. Without planning to, Aly leaned away from her older sister—knowing what she was capable of made being this close to her feel like she'd just heard a snake's rattle. But when Rachael leaned forward on her elbows and looked Aly square in the face, she did so wearing her typical calm, unimpressed expression.

"Aly, does this not seem like me? Do I seem like I'm being controlled by some sort of, whatever, alien parasite, or demonic possession?"

Aly looked into her sister's eyes, considering her answer, and . . .

"No," she said. "It seems like you. You're just . . ."

"I'm maybe a more complicated person than you thought I was," said Rachael with a slow nod. "That makes sense. If you read my diary, the things I've written in there might make your eyes bug out. But I need you to listen to me—the fire and me, we're one and the same. *I'm* in control. *I* wanted you to live out this story. And since that's not working out, *I* want to burn down the dance."

"But *why*?"

"I don't know. Because I'm angry at it," said Rachael with a shrug, flinging her arms out. "Because it's this stupid popularity game at school, and it's unfair, and puts a lot of pressure on girls our age. Because I didn't win. Because . . . I just do."

"But the night watchmen—any janitors hanging around, they—"

"It's an off night for the janitors," said Rachael. "I checked the schedule in the teachers' lounge. And the night watchman is asleep in his little security shed out back. I'll control the fire to keep it from spreading too far. I'm on top of this, Aly."

The information left Aly blinking in surprise. She

exhaled hard, and her shoulders lowered. Her sister had taken all the little details into account. She hated to admit it, but this was classic Rachael.

"So what's the story?" Aly said with a smile. "What are people in school going to hear when they find the gym in ashes?"

Rachael hissed through her teeth. She shot Aly a tight-lipped smile.

Aly didn't understand at first . . . and then it came over her like a wave of cold garbage on her heart.

"Oh," she said. "You're still pinning it on me."

"Yeah," said Rachael.

"You . . . *always* planned to pin it on me," said Aly, feeling the full weight of the realization hit her. "Before you got obsessed with me, back when this was the whole plan . . . you were always going to get me to take the fall. That's why you made them think I had the powers. Or, at the very least, really liked lighting fires."

"Yeah," said Rachael.

The sisters sat there in a moment of silence.

"If it's any consolation," said Rachael, "it wasn't

anything really personal. You just weren't doing a lot with your life anyway—"

Aly was out of the chair before she knew what was happening, tackling her sister to the ground with a scream.

INFERNO

The two girls rolled across the floor in a tangle of elbows and knees. Rachael seemed more startled than angry at first, as though fending off her sister's slaps and scratches was mostly just an unexpected bummer. That only made Aly burn hotter, knowing that Rachael never thought she had it in her. Now she felt the full force of her fire, the heat from her heart overpowering; these were the flames she'd felt before when she was sure it was her causing the accidents, controlling the fire. Maybe the powers had been Rachael's, but the anger had been hers.

"I hate you!" screamed Aly. "You've never cared about me and Simon! It was all only about yourself!"

"Prove me wrong, Als!" Rachael laughed. "Tell me about the time you made a difference."

Aly snarled and twisted until she was straddling her sister, pinning her arms down.

"How about now?" snapped Aly.

Rachael rolled her eyes.

In less than a second, Aly's braces turned burning hot, searing the insides of her lips.

She cried out and leaped off Rachael, opening her mouth in a horrible grimace to keep her lips from touching the metal inside them. She lurched to the table, grabbed the end of her sister's soda, and poured it on her red-hot teeth, wincing at the sizzling sound that came off her orthodontia.

The can in her hands ran hot. She shrieked, tossed it to the floor, and blew on her fingertips. Now both of her hands were burned.

The temperature began to rise noticeably. All around Aly, metal glowed in the darkness—the chairs, the legs of the folding tables, the stands holding up the backdrops and curtains. Aly watched in horror as the soda can on the ground began to dissolve into a bubbling pool of molten metal.

"Now, there's an idea," said Rachael in a hoarse, dark voice. "Maybe the gym doesn't burn down. Maybe it *melts* down."

Aly rushed to Simon and pulled him off his chair just as it began to tilt slightly on its glowing legs. Her brother snapped to, awoken from his weakened doze by her sudden movements. His eyes flickered around the room, taking in the drooping, dripping metal that surrounded them.

"We need to get out of here," said Aly, pulling him back toward the door—but they had taken barely a step before a table in front of them burst into flames.

Aly whirled and faced her sister. Rachael's face was twisted in a hateful scowl the likes of which Aly had never seen before, and she gently clawed her hands at her sides, as though drawing the heat to her. Her hair blew back from her face in the hot air, and as she walked slowly toward them, blasts of flame leaped off the glowing metal surfaces, like the fire was worshipping her as she passed.

And yet, even though Aly believed Uncle Marco, even though she knew the fire was turning up the heat inside her sister, she could still see Rachael behind those eyes. The anger and contempt there were feelings Aly had seen in her their whole lives.

She was right. She and the fire were one.

Aly clutched Simon to her, feeling the heat sting her face as more and more flames began to blast through the air and chairs and tables around them continued to droop and melt. The whole world was raging flame, molten metal, choking black smoke.

There was nowhere to go.

"Aly, I've . . . I think I've gotta do it," said Simon.

Aly gritted her teeth. Even after all this, the thought made her feel awful.

But he was right.

"I know," she said. "Do it."

"Sorry, Rachael," said Simon.

He tensed in Aly's arms.

Rachael's furious expression suddenly stopped.

One corner of her mouth stretched out to reveal clenched teeth. Then her whole body convulsed, bending and shaking in odd angles—until her hands went to her face, and she let loose a scream that made Aly squeeze her own eyes shut tight.

When she opened them, Rachael lay on the floor, one foot twitching slightly.

All at once, the fires around them exploded into the air. Paper flowers and cloth drapes burned wildly, letting out huge gouts of black smoke. Without Rachael to control it, Aly realized, the fire was doing what fire did—raging out of control.

"Come on!" Aly screamed, rushing to her sister's prone form. Simon weakly joined her, blinking hard and stumbling, and they each hooked one of her arms over their shoulders. As fast as they could, keeping low to avoid the smoke, they dragged their sister through the door, out of the cafeteria, and into the cold night air.

Once they were out on the football field, Aly laid Rachael down and looked at her. Her sister's face was totally dead, eyes open but glazed, mouth hanging limp. A trickle of blood ran out of her left ear.

Somehow, amid the heat coming off the school, a spike of cold rocketed through Aly. Her fingers flew to Rachael's neck, just below her jaw, like the doctors did on TV, and . . .

"She's alive," she gasped. "Her heart's still beating. She . . ."

Sobs swept over Aly. She bent over the limp body of her sister and wept. Simon put his arms around them both, and together they stayed, lit by their burning school and listening to the sounds of sirens growing in the distance.

ASHES

"Here we go," said Uncle Marco. Even through the downpour and the steady swipe of his windshield wipers, Aly could recognize the shape of the facility in the distance. The white block of narrow-windowed concrete had come to occupy a place in her heart as dark and dreary as the day they now drove through.

Marco pulled up front, and Aly said, "Thanks," and hopped out. She didn't even ask if he wanted to join her at this point; so far, with every visit, he'd shaken his head hard and peeled out of the parking lot. He said it was a proximity issue. *Can't be too close. Gotta stay in control.*

She walked in the front door and nodded to Nancy, the sour-faced old woman behind the desk, who waved her on in. Every hallway inside the facility looked the same—a starkly lit linoleum floor, five doors on either side, the occasional moan or scream coming from somewhere distant—but Aly had memorized the way and navigated herself to B Ward. Like she had on every visit, she nodded and smiled at the hospital staff she passed; this time, she also clutched the cylinder in her pocket and felt the rush of doing something bad and getting away with it. Invisibility had its perks.

Mikey, one of the orderlies, waited for her in front of Door 225. "Afternoon, Aly," he said.

"Hi, Mikey," she said softly. "Twenty minutes, I know."

The big man opened the door, and Aly walked into the white room. It smelled cleaner this time, like mint and chemicals. They must have cleaned it yesterday, on her off day.

"They don't even ask me for my name anymore,"

she said, pulling out the chair from the corner and sitting to face the bed. "It's like they think I'm cute for coming to see you all the time."

Rachael didn't budge. From where she sat propped up on her bed, Aly's big sister did the same thing she did every visit: stared at the wall. Her eyes were unblinking, her mouth hung limply open, and her hands sat lifeless in her lap. She was only sitting up because the nurses moved her for Aly's visit every other day. If she'd moved on her own in the two months since that night at the gym, Aly had never seen it.

"So, I have some good news: Mom and Dad have officially been cleared of all wrongdoing," she said. "The school accepted that they didn't know anything. I guess there were a couple of stories in your diary that Mom could back up. They sent out this stupid letter, though, basically telling all the other parents to stop bothering us. It indirectly confirms that our family was the problem, even if it says we weren't. People are angrier than ever.

"That diary . . . I don't know what we would've done without it, Rachael." Aly sighed. "It's a good thing you were so honest in it. I mean, obviously no one believed the stuff about, you know, your powers. They still say it's a delusional take on pyromania. But at least it let everyone know it wasn't me or Simon. That was a big help." She laughed a little. "I guess we also spilled all that lighter fluid in your room. They thought that was you."

Silence, except for the fluorescent lights buzzing overhead. Aly didn't know what she expected. The doctors said Rachael was gone. Wholly catatonic—and probably would be for the rest of her life. Apparently, a key section of her brain had suffered a massive hemorrhage. They had no idea what had caused it, but they knew it was devastating.

Aly didn't want to admit to herself that her big sister wasn't here anymore.

But it had been two months.

And every visit was the same.

Well, except for this one.

"I brought you something," said Aly. She pulled the scented candle out of her pocket and rolled it in her hands. The wax was golden with black dots, and the label on the glass jar that held it read CINNAMON BLISS with a picture of frosted cinnamon buns on it.

The scent of it instantly seemed to fill the room, its too-sweet aroma mixing with the harsh smell of cleaning fluid and making Aly feel a tiny bit nauseous.

"I don't know if this was one of your favorites or not," she admitted. "It was just the only one I rescued when Mom was throwing yours out. She went ballistic, just gutting your room. I think it was her way of dealing—"

A flash of a memory hit Aly—her mother's face, wide-eyed and panicked as she swept a whole dresser-top's worth of candles into a trash bag.

Aly's throat stung, and she tried to swallow the image down.

"I know I'm not supposed to bring you anything, and they'll probably take it away," she said, trying to avoid the tears. "But Dr. Bailey, my new therapist, thinks I need to make a peace offering to you. To help forgive you." The feelings hit Aly in a rush, and she let them go. "The thing is, I'm not sure I do forgive you. Not yet. Because even if I didn't get blamed, our lives are all messed up. Mom barely talks, and she cries every night, and Dad keeps slamming doors without being near them, and Simon has become this really intense kid at school and keeps getting in trouble, and it's all different because you care more about yourself than us—"

The pastry on the label went blurry in Aly's vision. She wept, letting the tears fall onto her sweatshirt. She'd done everything she could to be strong, but if this whole ordeal had taught her anything, it was that she had to let go sometimes. And given everything she was feeling, now seemed as good a time as any.

After she'd cried a bit, she wiped her face on her sleeve and stood. "I should go," she said. She placed the candle in her sister's cupped hands and swept some hair out of her face and over her ear. She wanted to say something else. Anything else, to reach her sister.

"The other day, I remembered how you taught me to dive," she blurted out. "At that vacation house we stayed in that one summer, with the pool. I was so freaked out, and you'd been so mean to me lately, but you were so cool about it then. You really took the time to teach me. I . . . Anyway. I wanted you to know I remembered that. I love you. I'll see you in two days."

As she left, Mikey gave her a tight, sad smile and pointed to the window in Rachael's door. "Just FYI,

I gotta take that thing away from her in a little bit. Sorry."

"I figured," said Aly with a nod. "I just wanted to bring her something from home. See if it helped. Pretty stupid, I guess."

"Nah, that's sweet," he said. "See you in a couple of days, Aly."

"Bye," she said, and headed down the hall, wondering if *sweet* meant *pitiful*, wondering why she even bothered visiting someone who was nowhere to be found.

A candle.

Somewhere in her, flint struck for the first time in a while.

A spark lit the darkness, if only for a second.

A candle. In my hands.

Crack. Again. The numb silence was blasted with light, movement, *heat*.

Aly brought me one of my candles.

The strikes landed steadily now, and faster. The sparks strobed through her, so that she could make out shape and motion. In the steady flashes, she saw an outline of her body, her mind, a life she'd had once.

Bringing her hands to her face hurt. Her joints ached. But with each spark, each flash of light, she willed it more, *more*, until the candle was under her nose, until her breath caught its scent and the sparks came faster, and from the depths of the darkness rose words she didn't recognize until they found their way into her mouth in a wave of pins and needles, and . . .

"Cinnamon Bliss," said Rachael hoarsely.

The spark caught.

Inside Rachael's mind, a flame blossomed, lighting up the space within her like a jack-o'-lantern. For the first time in two months, she blinked, and swallowed, and took in the world. She dragged in a deep breath of the candle's smell again, and it seemed to feed the fire, making it bloom with a halo of light.

With her flame relit, it all came back to her, like raising a torch to a cave painting. The school. Aly tackling her. Putting the flame into all the metal, making it glow hot and run boiling across the floor. Simon using his own gift against her, a sharp pain and sudden darkness that plunged her down to the bottom of her own mind.

She must have been gone long. Her eyes and muscles hurt. Her mouth was bone dry.

The fire, though, felt powerful. Stronger than ever, and very awake. While she'd been asleep, it had dug deeper into her, and now it was a part of everything around her. She could feel fire in everything, just waiting to be ignited. Every drop of water secretly wanted to boil. Every plank of wood ached to ignite, blacken, and scatter as ash. Only now, after her long absence, was she able to see how the fire was part of all things. An element, no different from earth, water, or air.

How long had she been gone?

She breathed the candle scent again.

Aly knew. Simon, too. They'd snuffed out the flame, after all.

Rachael wanted to have a serious talk with them about that. About lots of things.

The click of a lock being thrown.

Her eyes went to the door.

"All right, kiddo, gonna have to take that back,"

said the guard, swinging open her door. "Can't be letting you have—"

He saw Rachael's focused gaze, the candle held up to her nose. He froze, eyes bugging, hand still on the door handle.

Rachael found the heat in the metal of the door.

The guard screamed as the iron went molten in his hand. He staggered backward and collapsed, holding his shaking, burnt hand out in front of him and crying in pain.

She focused on the hinges. The metal glowed hot, then went soft. The door fell away, hitting the floor with a boom.

An alarm went off somewhere in the hospital. She heard shouts and oncoming footsteps. Rachael smiled, letting the fire show her where to focus, what to burn. If anyone tried to stop her, well, they'd know what it meant to get in her way.

Rachael closed her eyes and turned up the heat.

She'd be home in no time.

ACKNOWLEDGMENTS

As always, a heap of gratitude is due to David Levithan, my editor and friend, for continuing to believe in me and helping make this burning book a reality. Cheers, sir.

Many thanks to my agent, John Cusick, who is for some reason excited to work with a weirdo like me.

A bow of my head to Stephen King, whose novel *Carrie* was hugely inspirational in the writing of *Ablaze*. King of course also has a book named *Firestarter* that's thematically relevant to this one, but it was *Carrie* that really inspired me this time, and *'Salem's Lot* that got me here in the first place. Thanks, man.

To Azara, my love, and Jacob, my heart. Life is a desert at night, but you are my bonfire.

And finally, my eternal love to my brother, Quin, and my sister, Maria. Being the middle child between you two has taught me more about the world's beauty and strangeness than I could've ever imagined. Thank you for making me who I am.

ABOUT THE AUTHOR

Christopher Krovatin is an author and journalist whose YA and middle-grade novels include *Ablaze, Darkness, Red Rover, Heavy Metal & You, Venomous, Frequency*, and the Gravediggers trilogy. His work for publications including MetalSucks, *Kerrang!, Revolver*, The Pit, and Invisible Oranges have made him an expert on art that would make anyone feel like they could start a fire with their mind.

Chris currently lives in Bethlehem, Pennsylvania, with his wife, Azara, and their son, Jacob. He would love to know what you're going to be for Halloween.